ADINKRAHENE

ADINKRAHENE

Fear of a Black Planet

J. A. Faulkerson

J. A. Faulkerson Books

ADINKRAHENE
Fear of a Black Planet

A Novel by
J.A. Faulkerson

Second Printing

Cover illustrations by
Demar Douglas, The Painter of Dreams
www.demardouglas.com

Published by
J. A. Faulkerson Books
Culturally Coded Content
www.jafaulkerson.com

Follow me on Twitter at
https://twitter.com/bigvoice68

Friend me on Facebook at
https://www.facebook.com/jafaulkersonbooks

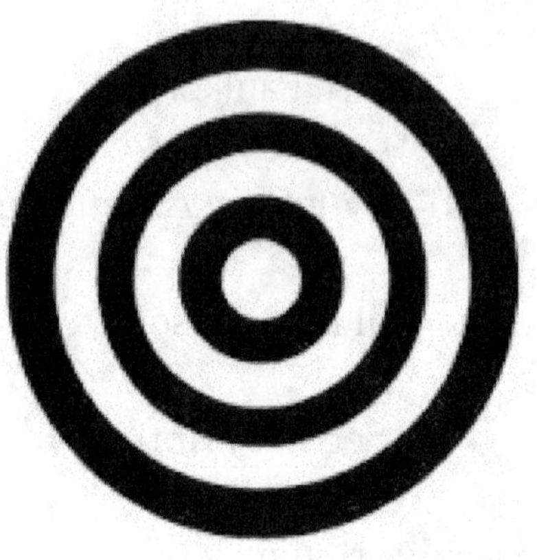

BOOK ONE
Fear of a Black Planet

IN A WORLD WHERE AMERICA HAS ELECTED ITS
FIRST, BLACK PRESIDENT, A NEW GENERATION OF
HEROES MUST EMERGE TO UNITE A DIVIDED KINGDOM.

When Mississippi Senator Kyle Shuler announces his bid to
unseat presidential incumbent Herbert Newsom, America's
first, black president, *Washington Post* political reporter
Jonathan Fraiser is miffed. He knows Senator Shuler's dirty,
little secret – that he and two of his friends murdered an
elderly, black woman as teenagers. But Jonathan isn't the only
person disturbed by Shuler's announcement. His longtime
friend Selina Giles, an FBI agent, was eleven years old when
Shuler slit her grandmother's throat. Now, Jonathan and
Selina must join forces as Adinkrahene agents to prevent a
Jim Crow criminal from becoming the leader of the free world.

Narrative of the Life of
Frederick Douglass
An American Slave
Unpublished Excerpt

April 19, 1843

I write this letter under the cloak of darkness. I am a free
man, an abolitionist, residing in the northern American states.
But now that I have gazed into the eyes of the enemy, I am
once again bound, by fear.

The enemy I speak of is not of this world. I can make this
claim because I traveled to their world through something my
green-skinned friend Daygon calls the Intergalactic Connector.
The Intergalactic Connector allows Satarians - that's what they
call themselves - to travel to and from other planets, teleport
away from detection or danger.

As I watched them from an underground Satarian overlook
– with Daygon by my side – I concluded that the Satarians are
vile creatures. Besides having green skins and forked tongues,
they also stand at least ten feet tall, both male and female.
Physiologically, their bodies resemble our own.

Daygon told me that his people were created by Lucifer, or
Satan, as full grown adults days after Adam and Eve were ex-
pelled from the Garden of Eden. The Satarian race was created
for the sole purpose of taking possession of the Earth to rule
over us, its inhabitants. I asked Daygon why his people did not
invade our planet immediately after our foreparents' expulsion

from Eden, and he said it was because of people who look like me, the descendants of Africa.

It was then that Daygon recounted mankind's origins. According to Daygon, Adam was created in God's image, from the dark African sands of Eden. Adam was a black man. Because there was no suitable helpmate for Adam, God created Eve from one of Adam's ribs. Because Eve came directly from Adam, she was black as well.

Supernatural forces were at work during Adam and Eve's residency in the Garden of Eden. Their first act of sexual intimacy in Eden caused a tidal wave of creative, electro-magnetic energy to cascade beyond Eden's borders and across the nation of Pangea. Adam's sperm and Eve's eggs mingled with Eden's embryonic sands to spread through the Pangean nation, producing multi-colored humans that spoke a common language. They would continue to speak this common language until God confounded them. They had disobeyed God by constructing a tower to get closer to Him. This construct came to be known as the Tower of Babel.

The Satarians' infiltration into human culture became more purposeful and strategic fifty years before the Babylonians built their tower to God. This was a time when everyone in Babel was united in thought and purpose. Its citizens also believed in the one, true God. But it was a time when embedded Satarians laid the groundwork for dividing and conquering the united Pangean nation. Lucifer reminded the most loyal members of his sect that a kingdom divided cannot stand.

Masquerading as lighter-skinned Babylonians, they convinced other lighter-skinned Babylonians that they were better than the darker-skinned ones. Thus began a race to the top, with the victorious racial group being allowed to offer up its own version of world history and humanity's relationship with the one, true God.

After God confounded their language and scattered them across the Earth, members of the lighter-skinned group committed themselves to ruling over their darker-skinned siblings. The Satarians in their midst provided them with the advanced weaponry they needed to subvert the darker-skinned groups. They were also able to create tools and devices that revolutionized the way humanity lived, worked and played. And if and when they saw something interesting that was created by members of the darker-skinned groups, they claimed it as their own.

Daygon said there are other residents on Sataria who do not want to invade Earth. They would much rather use the Intergalactic Connector to explore other planets in the universe. Taking such a position is considered blasphemy to the leaders of the Satarian Empire, for it is a demonstration of affection for the one, true God. Lucifer wants to prove to all creation that he is God's better. However, achieving this lofty goal was made even more difficult when many of the early blasphemers deserted his camp. They used their Intergalactic Connectors to escape Sataria and build peace-loving colonies on other habitable worlds.

My African brothers and sisters, I received confirmation from Daygon that we are God's chosen people, the instruments that God is using to thwart Lucifer's schemes. Daygon told me that Lucifer directed his minions to remove many of us from Africa so our minds would be fixated on our victimization and not on discovering the source of our strength.

That source is Eden, Daygon says. And it is located somewhere in Africa. Find it, and you will know power like you have never known before.

Our beautiful, black bodies are supernaturally linked to Eden. Therefore, I tend to believe our best days are ahead of us, not behind. The natural sons and daughters of Eden will rise up again to provide the charismatic leadership that this world needs to rebuild the Pangean nation. To rebuild the Beloved Community of equals.

Adinkrahene!

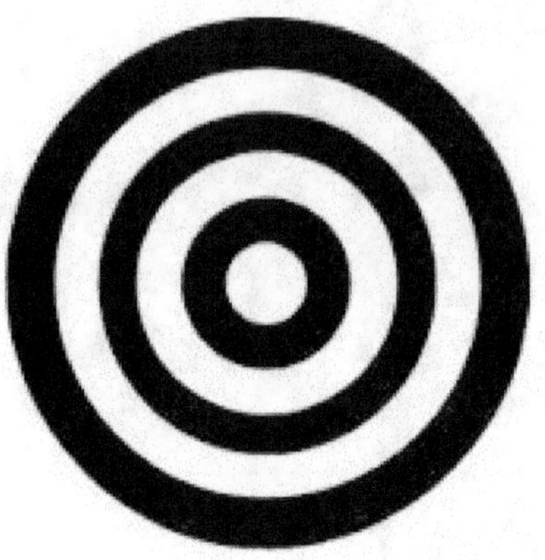

GUIDING PRINCIPLES OF AN ADINKRAHENE AGENT

WE descend from great, charismatic leadership.

WE commit to developing strong minds, strong bodies and strong spirits.

WE work diligently to rebuild the Beloved Community – the Pangean Nation.

WE reject any and all attempts to put profits over people.

WE give selflessly of our time, talent and treasure.

PROLOGUE

"Be quiet!" 17-year-old Kyle Shuler had exclaimed with a whisper. He, Roscoe Baker and Cleat McMullin were hiding behind a tree near the entrance to the Shuler family's sprawling estate. "Here she comes."

Sixty-four-year-old Mary Giles, a portly, African-American woman dressed in a white blouse and black skirt, made her way down the long driveway, black purse dangling from her bent arm. She had made this walk down from the Shuler's 10,000 square foot mansion to the Wilson Road bus stop outside the front gate at least five days a week. Once there, she caught the two or four o'clock bus home.

Normally, Ms. Mary, as she is affectionately called by Jackson residents, is accompanied by her best friend Adele Whitfield. But Adele had called in sick this hot summer day in June 1977. The other members of the Shuler's help staff were still up at the big house helping Kyle's mother, Linda, prepare for a Friday night dinner party. Ms. Mary wanted to get home ahead of her eleven-year-old granddaughter Selina. Selina had completed another successful year at Jackson, Mississippi's Frederick Douglass Elementary School, and Ms. Mary wanted to prepare a celebratory meal for her.

But as Ms. Mary had passed the boys, Kyle, Watson and Linda Shuler's oldest child, startled her by stepping onto the gravel road. His face was covered with a black stocking cap.

However, a quiet calm washed over Ms. Mary when recognition set in.

"Kyle," Ms. Mary had asked, "is that you?"

A masked Roscoe discreetly positioned himself behind Ms. Mary. A masked Cleat stood in the background, a few feet away from Kyle.

None of the boys said a word.

Ms. Mary had stepped closer to Kyle. She had been a Shuler family employee for over twenty years.

"It is you." Ms. Mary had said. "But what you doing out here walking the streets at one thirty in the afternoon. You s'posed to be at school, boy."

Kyle had removed his stocking cap. "Why'd you do it, Ms. Mary? Why'd you go tell on me?"

A long pause.

"'Cause your Ma and Pa would have been mad at me if I hadn't."

The two had just eyeballed each other after that. Kyle was consumed with the incident in question, the one that saw him consistently meeting up with his adopted sister Andrea for sexual romps in the family pool house. Ms. Mary, on the other hand, thought about the day she changed Kyle's diaper for the first time, how bad it smelled.

Kyle had pulled a switchblade knife from the back pocket of his jeans. He flipped it open to expose the six-inch blade inside. Then, in one motion, he plunged it deep into Ms. Mary's chest, inches from her heart. After he had pulled it out, Ms. Mary grabbed at her blood-soaked blouse.

"That's the problem with you niggers," Kyle had announced, "you done forgot who runs the show 'round here."

Roscoe then barreled into Ms. Mary's legs from behind, knocking her to the ground. Ms. Mary attempted to get back to her feet, but not before Kyle pulled her to him by her hair.

He forcibly tilted her head back, and then slit her throat with the knife.

Ms. Mary had fallen forward, withering in pain on the gravel road. As she lied there, a pool of blood expanded on the ground around her upper torso and head.

Kyle Shuler wiped at the tiny spots of foreign blood on his face. "Let's get out of here," he said to his friends.

With that, the boys returned to the woods. Cleat watched as Kyle and Roscoe transitioned from a trot to a sprint after stepping off the road. He, however, paused momentarily to glance back at a dying Ms. Mary.

"Forgive us, Lord," he had whispered. "Please forgive us."

He then stepped off the road in pursuit of his leader.

Within minutes of the boys' departure, a black Impala with shiny, chrome rims pulled up beside Ms. Mary's corpse. The back passenger door opened, and out stepped Watson Shuler, Kyle's father. Lit cigarette in hand, he had walked over to Ms. Mary's corpse. He then looked around with a restrained nervousness as two of his bodyguards fell in beside him.

"Put the body in their trunk," he had ordered as a second Impala pulled up beside the first one. "Dump it in the river, one hundred miles from here." He kneeled down to inspect the blank, open-eyed expression on Ms. Mary's face. "And have someone clean up this blood."

Watson had made his way back to the car. "Bitch got what she deserved," he had told his driver. "Don't need no nosy nigras up in here."

Watson slithered back into the back seat, and his driver closed the door behind him. As the car navigated past the crime scene and up the hill toward the mansion, Watson's other bodyguards busied themselves by placing Ms. Mary's corpse in a body bag.

CHAPTER 1
Jonathan Fraiser

I knew it was only a matter of time before my life took a turn for the worse, at least that's what I thought at first. I had just received word from my literary agent Sylvia Smalls that MSNBC's Lawrence O'Donnell wanted to interview me about my book *Middle Class Down: Thriving in America after The Great Recession*. I normally don't do interviews. I administer them as a journalist with the *Washington Post*. But Sylvia told me the only people who decline invitations to appear on *The Last Word* are Republicans.

I'm definitely not a Republican, or Democrat for that matter. If anything, I'm a pragmatist. When I cast votes in local, state and national elections, I usually cast them for candidates who believe in fairness for all. But back then, I was having a difficult time identifying these kinds of candidates. Modern-day politicos on both sides of the aisle had forgotten what it means to compromise.

My name is Jonathan Fraiser, but you can call me J. My mother always gets mad at me when I encourage people to do that because she named me Jonathan for a reason. She had named me after her father. But when I arrived in Washington, D.C. fifteen years ago to begin my new life as a political reporter with the *Post*, I wanted to mask my identity from my readers. If they wanted to know what the J and the A in J.A.

Fraiser stood for, they would have to do some digging on their own. I wasn't going to do the work for them. Didn't want some stranger tracking me down to get in my face to complain about something I wrote in one of my articles or books.

The topics I write about are in line with this country's populism. Around any water cooler in America, you will hear people talking about tightening our borders to stop the infiltration of illegal immigrants, extending tax cuts to Middle Class Americans, and making health care more accessible and affordable to working class Americans. But considering I'm an African American, I wanted to make sure my readers had an appreciation for how certain types of legislation adversely impact people of color, especially the ones that look like me.

Back in 2011, I was sitting in the Congressional press room, awaiting the arrival of Mississippi Senator Kyle Shuler. Senator Shuler had represented his state for close to four years, and many Republican strategists believed he would be the best person to put up against Democratic incumbent Herbert Newsom in the 2012 presidential election. Most prognosticators predicted that Shuler would lose. They believed President Newsom was doing right by America despite unrelenting opposition from the Republican-controlled House of Representatives.

I remember looking up from the front row to see Senator Shuler entering the room, displaying his trademark smile. His 25-year-old daughter Kelli, a recent Harvard graduate who he hired as his Communications Director, was by his side carrying an accordion file of important documents. As her father bounced onto the lectern to deliver his comments, she maneuvered past some cameramen to stand against the wall. She glanced over at me. I winked at her. But she stared through me, at Roscoe Baker, her father's Chief of Staff.

Senator Shuler adjusted the microphone for his height, and then tugged at his maroon tie. His black, tailor-made suit fit his trim physique like a glove. I, and other members of the Congressional press pool, leaned in as Shuler prepared to speak.

"I want to thank you, members of the worldwide press, for being here today," Shuler began. "As you all know, I never thought I'd enter the world of politics. My father, Watson Shuler, represented us well as Mississippi governor. But after three years in congressional office, my feelings have changed.

"While I, and members of the Republican Party, applaud President Herbert Newsom for being the first African American to occupy the Office of the Presidency, I personally feel his policies have done nothing to create new jobs and improve our ailing economy. I also disagree with the Supreme Court's recent decision, which declared President Newsom's immigration legislation constitutional. By crafting such a radical piece of legislation, he and the Democratic Party have opened this country up to domestic terrorist attacks from foreign extremists.

"That's why I have come here today to share my heart, and make a major announcement. I love this country, the people who call it home. I believe in freedom, in liberty. But I can't stand idle when our president's policies destroy our way of life. Therefore, I am here today to formally announce my bid to seek and secure the American presidency."

Shuler's announcement brought about a verbal explosion. Hands went up, questions were blurted out. Shuler called on Melanie Matthews, an attractive, 30-something, Caucasian correspondent with CNN, to ask the first question. I exchanged a knowing glance with Harvey Clemons, a CBS cameraman, who was eyeballing Melanie's tanned legs.

"Jonathan," Harvey whispered, "Is it just me, or is Melanie's skirt two inches shorter than it was last week?"

I covered my mouth with my hand to muffle a chuckle. I looked away from Melanie's crossed legs to catch Kelli staring at me again. She quickly directed a scrunched up brow at me before returning her attention to her father.

"Senator Shuler," Melanie began. "Glad to hear about your candidacy. But what do you think your chances are when so many Americans disagree with your stance on immigration. Sixty-seven percent of the Americans polled in a recent CNN/New York Times poll applaud President Newsom for taking the necessary action to keep the American dream alive for immigrant children brought here by their parents."

Shuler interrupted. "And a poll administered by the Heritage Foundation discovered that ninety-five percent of their respondents believe his Executive Order is nothing but a ploy to get more of the Hispanic vote."

"With that being said then," Melanie continued, "how would you address immigration? These children haven't done anything wrong. Many of them have been living in this country all their lives. Shouldn't they be allowed to become American citizens?

"Yes, they should. But not at the expense of our native citizens." He sighed, carefully considering his words. "I would repeal President Newsom's order; replace it with something that is more permanent. I just think stop-gap measures like this one are sending the wrong message to foreigners who want to relocate to this country."

I couldn't agree more. To me, his position was in lock step with voter sentiment. Most Americans have already been balking at the corporate sector's tendency to hire illegal immigrants as a form of cheap domestic labor. And with the tax code benefiting companies that ship jobs overseas, most Americans are tired of living in communities where even decent jobs are hard to come by.

Senator Shuler took a few more questions. As these questions are being asked, I scanned the room, occasionally scribbling short-hand notes on my notepad. My digital voice recorder captured Shuler's full comments. But as Shuler stepped off the lectern and exited the room with Kelli and

Baker in tow, I spotted an old friend, leaning against one of the marble pillars near the back of the crowded room. Her blue pants suit accentuated the lines of her tall, voluptuous body. Kind of reminded me of black actress Pam Grier as Foxy Brown from back in the day.

"Funny seeing you here," I said to this old friend in the hallway after wading through the press corp. "What's the FBI doing in the halls of Congress? Aren't you supposed to be out in the field bringing bad guys to justice?"

My old friend smiled.

"Hello, J," she replied. "Glad to see you haven't lost your sense of humor."

I placed my leather briefcase on the marble floor. I then leaned forward to embrace her, kiss her on the cheek. "Glad to see the years have been kind to you, Selina." I stepped back to look her over. "You haven't changed one bit. Still looking fabulous."

"You're not too shabby yourself," Selina replied. "You still working out at the Y, or have you upgraded to 24-Hour Fitness. Looks like you're still rocking a six pack under that suit jacket."

"More like a four pack," I replied, "Hectic travel schedule. I'm lucky to get three in a week." I realized that she was looking at the ring finger on my left hand. "Yeah, she left me about three years ago. Got tired of coming home to an empty house."

"I'm so sorry, J," Selina consoled. "Thought you and Carmelita were so right for each other." She abruptly switched the subject. "You available for dinner tonight, or do you have a deadline to meet?"

"Yes. But I can always make time for you...I mean the FBI."

"How about Sweet Georgia Brown's at six?"

I checked the time on my watch.

"Make it seven, and I'm good."

"Seven it is. See you there."

As Selina made her way down the front stairwell, I caught myself admiring her backside. Baby girl still had back after all those years. In my mind, Selina looked as good as she did during our days at the University of Tennessee, when I was a point guard on the men's basketball team, she a world-class sprinter on the women's track and field team.

While at Tennessee, I majored in Print Journalism, with a minor in Political Science. Selina was notorious for staying up late to watch reruns of *Hawaii Five O*, so no one was surprised when she announced she would be majoring in Criminal Justice with a minor in Psychology. As student-athletes, we both had whirlwind schedules the moment we stepped on campus. So, the only time we would see each other was during meal times, in the cafeterias at Gibbs Hall or the Presidential Court Complex. And even though she wasn't my lady, I still considered her one of my closest friends.

I had a reputation of being a quiet, reserved brother with shifty eyes. Yes, I would laugh at my teammate's jokes, but I wasn't likely to initiate them. But all that changed when Selina sat in an empty chair between her boyfriend Brian "Bank Shot" Banks and me. Once she was seated, she bumped into my shoulder, and then accused me of being "one of them uppity Negroes."

"Uppity?" I had replied. "Girl, please!"

Truth be told, Selina's accusation was flattering. If I hadn't known better, I would have thought she was flirting with me. But she and Bank Shot had been in a steady relationship for the past three years. She obviously wasn't going to end this relationship when real money was on the line.

At seven two, Bank Shot was the team's senior captain. More importantly, he was projected to be one of the top picks in the 1987 NBA Draft. Selina was indeed going to take her shot at becoming an Olympian, but she wanted the riches that Bank Shot earned in the NBA to be her ticket to a more, privileged life.

Selina had directed my attention to her seated teammates on the other side of the dining hall.

"See the new girl, the one over there in the corner?" I had nodded as I recognized Carmelita sitting at the end of the table. Carmelita had looked up then away when she realized we were eyeballing her. "She thinks you're cute. Just doesn't know how to approach you. Said you always looking like you in deep thought or something."

"I'm not into freshmen, Selina. You know that."

"But she's not a freshman, J. She's a sophomore. Recent transfer from East Tennessee State."

Bank Shot had interjected with a whisper, "She's a looker, J. You better get to her 'fore one of these knuckleheads get to her first." He had paused, and then shook his head. "Hell, if you don't watch it, I may have to whisper a few sweet nothings in her ear."

Selina had elbowed Bank Shot in his side. "You better face forward, Negro, 'fore you wind up with a fat lip."

The couple had shared a brief laugh before Bank Shot kissed Selina on the forehead, cheeks and lips. As she had rested her head on Bank Shot's chest, the look on her face let me know she was serious. But I also sensed she knew Bank Shot's remark was a sign that their relationship was destined to fail.

"We were through two years into our marriage," Selina exclaimed. "Found out he had been cheating on me when the Bulls were on the road. One of his tricks gave him herpes."

We were seated at a table in Sweet Georgia Brown's Soul Food Restaurant. Smooth jazz emanated through the room as patrons either claimed or relinquished their tables. I was pleased to see that Selina had changed from her pant suit to a yellow and white summer dress with a low-hanging front. Selina smiled when she spotted me staring at her rack.

"That had to hurt," I replied. My tongue took another swipe at the rib meat lodged in my back teeth.

"You haven't changed one bit." Selina tugged at the top of her dress. "Those eyes of yours are still as shifty as ever."

I chuckled as I rested my arms on the table.

She continued, "I always liked you, J. I know I used to give you a hard time about being so quiet, but you were always good to me. I think of you often, you know?"

"Really?"

"Yes. Really. I even subscribed to the *Post* when the Bureau relocated me to Los Angeles. You're an excellent writer. Loving your new book. It is opening my eyes to how unchecked power corrupts."

"Glad to hear that," I said, leaning in. "But I know you didn't invite me here just to talk about my book. What's up?"

Selina breathed in deeply. "I'm living in D.C. now, J," she whispered. "Been here two weeks. Working a new assignment. Cold case division." She took another deep breath. "That's why I'm here, J. We just reopened one of those cases, the one I told you about at UT."

"The one involving your grandmother?"

"Yeah."

"Well, you're going to be fighting an uphill battle, girl. I pro-filed Shuler for the *Post*, remember? When his father Watson retired from the Senate. The man is squeaky clean."

"But no one has ever been able to explain how my grand-mother's body was pulled from the river in Montgomery when she had just gotten off work in Jackson. Remember, she never got on that two o'clock bus, J. Two and half months passed before they found her body."

I noticed tears welling up in Selina's eyes. "I was invited to the press conference as one of their special guests. But I'm tired of maintaining this façade, like everything is alright be-tween us. It's not. I'm just trying to keep my enemies closer than my friends. Did his announcement surprise me? Hell, yeah, it did. But I should have seen it coming." Selina breathed in deeply as she used her napkin to wipe at her eyes. "This new assignment gives me the resources and authority to take him down, J. I'm also aligned with a group that believes better days are ahead for people like you and me. We just need a little help from a political insider. You game?"

Selina placed her napkin back on the table.

She continued, "The American Dream – the pursuit of life, liberty and happiness – is nothing but a façade, J. A façade that has been created to keep us in check, line the pockets of rich white men. Taking the Shulers' down gets us one step closer to exposing what my benefactor calls the Corporate Cabal."

Selina then reached into her purse to pull out a metallic business card with aluminum wording and graphics. She placed it on the table in front of me.

"What's this?" I asked, studying the card. On one side of the card was the image of one, smaller, red circle inside two larger ones. A telephone number was centered in black on the other side.

"Call that number," Selina exhorted as she stood. "With your help, Kyle Shuler will finally pay for what he did to my grandmother." Then, as she turned to leave, "We know it as the Adinkrahene symbol. Google it when you get home. Once you take this first step, our hope is you will be more open to what we have to say."

CHAPTER 2
Kelli Shuler

I had been doing my best to avoid Jonathan, but I must admit it felt good seeing him at Daddy's press conference. When I saw him, memories of our time together flashed through my mind. That last time, when we were walking along the pier in Ocean City, Maryland, was special. For the first time in our month-long affair, I had felt a real connection with him. But this connection was nothing more than that – a feeling. Jonathan Fraiser just couldn't handle being with a young, intelligent white woman.

And I hate him for that.

Yes, he was 43, I 25. But when he told me that I should be dating men closer to my age, I wanted to slap him across his face. I told him right then and there that I am a "grown-ass woman," but he wasn't buying it. Dropping me was probably convenient for him. I wasn't surprised to see him talking with Selina in the hallway after Daddy's press conference.

I should have followed Daddy's advice. He never knew that Jonathan and I were sleeping with each other. If he did, he probably would have had a fit. Daddy is a by-product of the Old South. He would rather I mix it up with the young, male senators and representatives that frequented the Blair House Country Club. Of course, I would have had a problem with that. Hanging out with guys who place the health of their investment portfolios above me is not my cup of tea.

I always knew Jonathan wasn't getting rich down at the *Post*. Last I heard that rag's top reporters were making around $70,000 a year. But he is one of the most respected journalists in the business. When my Pa-Paw, Watson Shuler, retired from the Senate, Jonathan wrote an excellent piece on him that chronicled his four terms as Mississippi senator and two terms as Mississippi governor. It was during the interviews he conducted in Jackson with members of my family that we met.

I was impressed by his kind demeanor and good looks. My folks, however, were enamored by his celebrity. Jonathan Fraiser will always be remembered as the Tennessee Volunteer shooting guard who took it to the Ole' Miss Rebels in the 1990 Southeastern Conference Men's Basketball Championship Game. With five point four seconds on the clock, Jonathan reportedly faked a jump shot before stepping behind the three-point line to sink a three. The Vols won 61-59, advancing to the first round of the NCAA tournament.

"They give that man too much credit," Daddy complained as we entered his office in the bowels of the Russell Senate Office Building. "Newsom and the goddamned Democrats are the problem, not us." He strode to the other side of his mahogany desk to sit in his plush, leather chair. "Kelli, mark my word: Herbert Newsom is going to regret signing that Executive Order."

I replied, "I agree. It was a stupid thing to do. More Republicans should have been at the table. Immigration is supposed to be a bipartisan issue."

Roscoe Baker, my father's longtime friend, confidante and Deputy Chief of Staff, strode into the room. I sat in one of the four chairs surrounding a rectangular, mahogany table. As I did, I strained to read the business card in his right hand.

On the side facing me, I briefly saw the word "We" written in blue ink.

"Kelli, can you give us a minute?" Mr. Roscoe said with deep concern.

I stood. "Sure. Just let me know when you're done. I still have some questions about the highway bill."

"Sure thing."

While at my desk, I repeatedly peered over the top of my computer monitor, sneaking glances at them as they talked on the other side of the glass, behind a closed door. Mr. Roscoe was more animated than usual. Daddy sat behind his desk with a contemplative expression on his face. At first, I surmised that their discussion centered around Congress' low poll numbers. But when Mr. Roscoe waved the card inches from Daddy's face, I realized they never stopped talking about the card.

Daddy's office door swung open, and there he was, standing in the doorway.

"Kelli," he said. "Come on back in here, doll?"

When we're all holed up in his office, Daddy continued.

"You still corresponding with that black reporter down at the *Post*?" he asked.

"You mean, Jonathan?" I replied.

"Yeah, that's him," Mr. Roscoe interrupted.

Daddy rolled his eyes at his friend before looking back at me.

"If we're going to win this election," he continued, "we'll need the help of some good Nigras." He breathed in deeply. "I need you to draw that boy out in conversation a little more. Determine if he's conservative, liberal, or somewhere in the middle."

"Why?"

"Because of this."

With a nod of his head, he invoked Mr. Roscoe to hand me the business card that he held in his right hand. Daddy simultaneously pulled a stack of others from his desk drawer.

He spread them out near the front of his desk like a deck of playing cards.

I learned that the word following "We" is "know". I flipped it over to see what appeared to be a symbol – a smaller red circle surrounded by two larger ones.

"Got some nigras playing mind games with me, honey," Daddy continued. "Trying to deter me from running for President. But it's not going to work."

"But what does any of this have to do with Jonathan?"

"Probably nothing," Mr. Roscoe interjected. "But he may help us draw them out into the open. He may also know what this symbol means."

I took a second look at the symbol. "I've seen it before, down at the Smithsonian, back in 2006, during Pa-Paw's retirement party. If I'm not mistaken, it's some kind of African symbol. But I forget what it means." I retrieved the stack of cards from Daddy's desk, reading the backs of each one. They all said the same thing – We know!

"Glad to see Selina showed up," Mr. Roscoe added. "Didn't get a chance to speak with her. She looked pissed. May want to see if she can make heads or tails out of this one."

"Yes." Daddy snuck a glance at me before returning his attention to Mr. Roscoe. "Do that. She has always been a reliable foot soldier."

Daddy then sat behind his desk, hands folded. His demeanor unsettled me. His eyes came to rest on me. "We need you to charm Fraiser's socks off, Kelli. There are plenty of conservative-minded Nigras out there, Nigra's who feel Newsom's economic policies are wrong for America. A respected Nigra reporter like Jonathan could help us make the case for why Nigra voters should vote for me."

I winced at the thought of misleading Jonathan just so he would work on my father's behalf. But my family had a legacy to leave behind, and I was willing to do my part to preserve it.

Thaddeus, my African-American driver, opened the limousine door for me as I exited the Senate building. He greeted me with a head nod as I passed in front of him to get into the back seat. He had been my driver for over four years, a graduation gift from my father. I appreciated these kinds of gifts, because I didn't have an appetite for driving home after five in all that congestion. My hope then was the traffic wouldn't be that thick once we merged onto the freeway. With my watch registering nine fifteen p.m., many of the commuters should have been sitting comfortably in the homes by now, watching the Redskins/Cowboys game.

Thaddeus and I didn't say much to each other. We never did. But when I wanted to deviate from the route that took us to my penthouse apartment in Georgetown, I usually called him an hour in advance to let him know. But that night, I opted to stay the course. I just wanted to get home, take a Jacuzzi bath, dry off, lotion up real good, and then lie naked on my linen bed sheets as an old black and white movie played in the background.

I scrolled through the day's CNN newsfeed on my smartphone as Thaddeus weaved the limousine through traffic.

CHAPTER 3
Jonathan Fraiser

After taking a hot shower and slipping into my pajama bottoms, I plopped into the rolling chair in my home office, and pressed the power button on my laptop. The anticipation of learning more about the Adinkrahene symbol was getting to me.

Of all the African Adinkra symbols, Adinkrahene is chief among them. Three words that are associated with it are greatness, charisma and leadership. Sounds great, but I still wasn't seeing the correlation between it and Kyle Shuler.

I walked over to the kitchen island to retrieve the card that Selina gave me. I returned to my office, comparing the image on the card with the one on the computer screen. They were identical. I then flipped the card over to take another look at the telephone number.

I noted that the number had seven digits, not ten. If I made this call, there was no way of knowing the area that I called. I plucked my cordless phone from its cradle and then punched in the numbers. Three rings, a clicking sound, followed by what appeared to be a computerized female voice on the other end.

"State your first and last name, please," the computerized voice commanded.

"Jonathan Fraiser," I replied.

More clicking sounds on the other end.

"Welcome to the A-R-M-S Network, Mr. Fraiser," the computerized voice continued. "Thank you for following through with Agent Giles' instructions." More clicking sounds. "You are one step closer to having the answers that you seek. But before we proceed, are you in or out?"

I was somewhat reluctant to give an answer. Here I was talking to a computer, and I'm being asked if I was in or out.

"I'm in," I replied.

More clicking sounds.

The computerized voice then asked, "Do you have pen and paper?"

I opened my desk drawer to grab a ball point pen and a stack of sticky notes.

"Yes, I do."

"Your questions will be answered at..."

I scribbled the Potomac, Maryland address, as well as the meeting date and time, on the sticky note. The computerized voice provided this information two more times, and then the call was dropped.

I had visited Potomac on numerous occasions, usually to conduct interviews with legislators, judges, diplomats and lobbyists. I knew whomever lived at this address was a person of immense power, profound influence.

"Jonathan Fraiser," I told the black, front gate security guard from the driver's seat of my Honda Accord. He stood next to the driver side door holding a clipboard with the day's scheduled appointments. "I'm here for a six o'clock,"

"Yes, Mr. Fraiser," the security guard replied. "Mr. Black is expecting you. Please pull forward after I open the gate. Once you pass through the gate, just follow the paved road to the rotary in front of the mansion entryway. Mr. Wallace, the butler, will greet you there."

If I had known I would be meeting with world-renown inventor and venture capitalist Cornelius Black, I would have dressed it up a little more. But there was no turning back. I just hoped he didn't feel slighted because of my semi-casual dress – white t-shirt, black slacks and dress shoes. At least I had the foresight to hang my hounds tooth jacket in the backseat. But considering Mr. Black has been seen in the company of Jay-Z and Diddy, I thought he would give me kudos for looking so hip.

For all intents and purposes, Cornelius Black was a freak of nature, at least that's the moniker *Black Enterprise* magazine attached to him back in 1998. He had secured a sixty-five percent stake in Holodeck Systems, Incorporated, a black-owned CGI firm based in Van Nuys, California. Mr. Black was the first to recognize that the company was primed to further revolutionize how Hollywood movies were being made. So after Holodeck Systems supplanted George Lucas' Industrial Light and Magic three years later as innovators in CGI technology, he directed his mostly African-American staff of computer engineers, programmers and designers to create holographic conferencing devices for the corporate sector.

Today, these holographic devices can be seen hanging from the ceilings of many corporate conference rooms, smaller devices in employee offices. American businessmen use this technology to communicate with holographic representations of their staff members in North and South America, Europe and other parts of the world. I even learned that Holodeck Systems would be rolling out a version for home users in the Fall.

I stepped out of the car, and found myself being amazed at all the material wealth Cornelius Black has amassed. He was the world's richest man, succeeding oil magnates Harmon and Nigel Bain. The main building on Mr. Black's sprawling estate, the one that I entered, stretched as far as my eyes could see. And the entryway was reminiscent of a five-star hotel, not a private residence.

Pretty impressive for a fellow descendent of African slaves.

I walked up to the ornate, oak door and pressed the doorbell. The door swung open within seconds.

"Welcome, Mr. Fraiser," Mr. Wallace, a much older African-American gentleman dressed in a black tuxedo with tails, said. He waved his left arm forward and then backwards, inviting me to join him inside the mansion. "Mr. Black is out back." I stepped inside. "He is looking forward to meeting you. Follow me."

We exited the mansion through a rear door to step on the stone floor of the back patio. I saw Mr. Black sitting in the foreground at a glass-topped table with gold and silver trim. He sported a pair of Oakley sunglasses, and was dressed in white athletic shorts, a white Holodeck t-shirt and white K-Swiss sneakers. Centered on the table was a glass container filled to the brim with sweet tea, and a bowl of assorted fruit. Two tall glasses with ice and napkins, silverware and saucers lied at the ready on opposite ends of the table.

"Mr. Fraiser!" Mr. Black greeted as he stood. "Glad you could pencil me in. I pray you didn't have any problems finding the place."

I extended my hand only to have it consumed and vigorously shaken by Mr. Black's. My gaze shifted from him to the panoramic view of Washington. "No, sir," I replied. "No problems at all. Thank you for the invitation. And please, just call me Jonathan."

He then directed me to sit across from him at the table. As I pulled at my chair, I found myself admiring the man's physique. Sixty-four years old and in the best shape of his life. Everyone knows that back in 1964, he was one of the first African Americans to play on a Division One collegiate football team. But maintaining this level of fitness at his age was pretty impressive.

Both of our chairs were angled toward the city. I expressed envy about his being able to wake up every morning to such a view. I also commended him for being named *Time* magazine's Person of the Year for his philanthropic work in the U.S. and Africa. He reportedly used money from his own coffers to build fifty fully-funded K-12 schools in five years. Five thousand children attended the first ten alone. Mr. Black reminded me that he attributes his success to the many sacrifices of our African and African-American forebears.

Growing tired of the small talk, I abruptly told him that I followed Selina's instructions. "But what does it all mean?" I asked. "Adinkrahene? A-R-M-S?"

"It's all very simple, Jonathan," Mr. Black replied. "The Adinkrahene Reparations Management Syndicate, or ARMS, is all about returning the African Diaspora to global prominence. It's about securing reparations from the American government for centuries of institutionalized slavery and oppression. And in the case of Mary Giles and others, it's about finally being able to bring Jim Crow criminals to justice."

"But what are its origins?" I angled my chair toward Mr. Black and then rested my elbows on the table. "And what do you expect me, a journalist, to do to support its efforts?"

"We want you to do what you do best, Jonathan. Write. Write about Kyle Shuler's positions on taxation, education, immigration, healthcare, jobs and the economy. Ask the kind of questions other reporters are afraid to ask. Get working and middle-class Americans to see how our democracy has been hijacked by what Adinkrahene calls the Corporate Cabal."

"What do you mean? Corporate Cabal?"

"A group of mostly white, Anglo-Saxon Protestant businessmen whose only purpose is to implement and regulate the forces that reinforce Anglo superiority, minority inferiority. Their plot to control these forces was hatched even before Lyndon B. Johnson signed the Civil Rights Act of 1964."

"And you know this how?"

"Through a critical analysis of this country's history of African-American exploitation. Back in the day, these white businessmen exploited our ancestors by not paying them for their labor. During the Jim Crow era, they exploited them through dead-end jobs and low wages. Today, they have a vice grip on amateur and professional sports programs. While our black athletes are being compensated nicely for their efforts, members of the Corporate Cabal still walk away with close to three quarters of the profits.

"But their most damning scheme involves the privatization of the prison industrial complex. We African Americans make up 12 percent of the general population, yet represent over 50 percent of those incarcerated in federal prisons. No race of people can be exploited like that and emerge free of emotional scars, Jonathan. Adinkrahene exists to do what the NAACP, the SCLC, the SNCC and the NUL have been unwilling and unable to do. Return Africans and African-Americans to their rightful thrones."

Mr. Black stood.

"Follow me," he admonished. "There is so much more to see."

Mr. Black led me down a spiral, granite staircase surrounded by granite walls with more ornate carvings on them. When we reached the bottom, he opened a section of the wall on his right to reveal a retinal scanning device. I watched as a wide beam of light swept over his right eye. A portion of the wall immediately slid away.

We walked down a long hallway as the entrance closed shut behind us. To our left and right were plate glass windows that ran the length of the hallway. Through one of the windows, I spotted two Adinkrahene agents, both black, sitting in cubicles hovering over computer terminals. Three other black agents – two males, one female – sat at a table in the back of the room chatting with the holographic projections of two, black female colleagues. I was amazed at how close the holograms resembled their flesh and blood originals.

Mr. Black stopped, affording me the time I needed to look around.

"This here is one of our operation centers." He pointed at the two black agents staring at the computer monitors. "From here, and our bases in Africa, Europe, the Middle East and Australia, we discreetly manipulate the flow of currency. The two men over there are hackers, probably the best in the business. Never knew a computer system they couldn't gain access to."

Mr. Black directed my attention to the holographic conferencing session. "They're finalizing plans for a new sting operation in the United Kingdom." A slight pause. "Adinkrahene's reach expands the globe, my friend. The money that we have leveraged to date from international corporations with ties to the slave trade will exceed fourteen trillion dollars by the end of twenty twelve."

"What will those funds be used for?" I asked.

"Reparations, of course."

"To whom?"

"You. Me. People who look like us. But we won't be depositing monies into individual banking accounts, or cutting individual checks. No. We're going to use it to revitalize communities of color in America first. And because Africa is the cradle of civilization, we will open a separate account to gain control of some of its most sought after resources."

"But why? Hasn't the American government done enough to atone for white peoples' sins?"

Mr. Black head snapped toward me as a smirk appeared on his dark face.

"You and I both know it hasn't. Yes, its most progressive citizens – of all hues – did rally together in two thousand and eight to elect the first black president. But the conservative ones, the ones with the most racist of views, are intent on making Herbert Newsom a one-term president."

He continued. "None of the white presidents that preceded Newsom ever apologized for slavery, or Jim Crow. They create reservations for Native Americans, and allow them to operate casinos on protected land. They offered sanctuary to the Jewish survivors of the Holocaust. But they tried to wipe the black race's pain away with desegregation measures. That's not good enough for me, Jonathan. They owe us more than that. If they're not going to pay up, we have no choice but to take what is owed to us."

"But aren't you concerned about getting caught?"

"No. I'm not. Not when I consider the ancestors who endured twenty or more lashes from metal-tipped whips. Not when I flick through the annals of American history and see photographs of our ancestors hanging by their necks from trees. No, I'm not concerned, Jonathan. If anything, I'm more determined than ever to right an injustice that has gone unchecked."

Mr. Black folded his arms. "Most people, when they're talking politics, think the game is about the interplay between Republicans, Democrats and Independents, Conservatives, Liberals and Progressives. They're wrong. The political bodies that matter are clustered closer to the color line, white versus black and everything in between. The Corporate Cabal would want us to believe that white is pure, incorruptible. Black the complete opposite – impure, corrupt. That's how they keep us in bondage, Jonathan. Adinkrahene is here to show members of the Black Diaspora how to break free of their shackles once and for all."

He unfolded his arms, sliding his hands into the pockets of his shorts. I leaned against the plate glass wall, stroking my goatee with my right hand as I processed his words. I had to give the man credit; he was a doer not a talker. But I cringed at the thought of being locked up for being associated with an organization that takes from the rich and gives to the poor. Like everyone else, I rooted for Robin Hood and his merry band of men, but serving a prison sentence wasn't that appealing to me.

"What do you want me to do?" I asked, pushing away from the wall to stand upright with my arms crossed.

"Help us bring Kyle Shuler crimes out into the open," Mr. Black replied. "We received confirmation about a year and a half ago that he was the one who murdered Mary Giles. An initiation rite devised by his father, Watson Shuler, to usher him and two of his friends – Roscoe Baker and Cleat Mc-Mullin – into the Cabal. Kyle and Roscoe were eighteen, Cleat seventeen."

"Who was the source?"

"Cleat McMullin. One of our agents on assignment at the Adam's County Correctional Center, in Jackson, got him to talk. Must have had a heart-to-heart meeting with Jesus. Told Agent Miles everything. Said Shuler slit Ms. Mary's throat."

Mr. Black continued, saying, "I understand your reluctance, Jonathan. I too had to think twice when Herbert Newsom invited me into the fold more than twenty years ago."

My mouth dropped.

"President Newsom has ties to Adinkrahene?"

"Yes. He came up with the new design for the RMS. I perfected it. As the former President and CEO of Legacy Bank and Trust, the Adinkrahene Council of Elders knew he was the right person to coordinate this effort. The man is a financial genius. And believe me when I say this; Herbert Newsom is the first African-American president because the Adinkrahene Syndicate fully supported his candidacy."

Mr. Black chuckled as he watched me shake my head in disbelief.

He continued, "I know it's a lot to process. But what do you think? You still in?'

"Sure," I replied with some reluctance. "I'm a child of The Movement. Feels good knowing there are still brothers out there fighting the good fight."

He patted me on the back. "No doubt, young blood." He then extended his arm toward a door on the other side of the hallway. "No doubt."

We entered a circular-shaped room that was reminiscent of a library, decorated with antique chairs and tables. Antique book shelves with classical and contemporary titles hugged the walls. Paintings of Frederick Douglass, W.E.B. Dubois, Marcus Garvey and Martin Luther King, Jr. were perched high on these same walls. I noticed other casually dressed Blacks – both male and female – sitting at the tables sprinkled throughout the spacious room. And to my right, I saw a mahogany door with a glass window and the words "Computer Lab" on it.

"This is our reading room," Mr. Black said as we approached an older, bespectacled, black female siting at an oval-shaped desk. "We have gone to great lengths to preserve anything written about or by the four men you see hanging on these walls, as well as other African and African-American authors both past and present." He slapped the top of the checkout counter. "And this here is Ms. Ruth Jackson, our historian slash librarian."

Ms. Jackson stood.

"Hello, Cornelius," she said. She extended her hand to me. "And hello to you, Mr. Fraiser."

I shook and released her hand, surprised that someone I've never met knew my name.

She continued. "I've been following your career for quite some time. Your new book is pretty popular around here. I'd be surprised if we still have a copy on the shelf. Had to order ten more just to meet agent demand."

"Music to my ears," I quipped.

Mr. Black interjected, "Ruth isn't telling you everything, Jonathan. Selina had a lot to do with your being here today, but Ms. Jackson here endorsed the idea."

"We just thought he would be an asset to the Shuler sting, Cornelius. With his being a member of the Congressional press pool, Senator Shuler won't expect a thing."

"And that's why I love you, Ruth," Mr. Black replied.

Mr. Black then left me in Ms. Jackson's capable hands. Ms. Jackson and I retreated to one of the adjacent conference rooms, and she brought me up to speed on Adinkrahene history, occasionally directing my attention to the images of Civil Rights heroes and sheroes on the LCD screens lining the far wall.

According to Ms. Jackson, the Adinkrahene Syndicate first came to prominence in 1932, at the height of The Great Depression and the subsequent second World War. It was the brainchild of Rufus T. Hancock, a Tuskegee airman. Hancock loved America, but he hated the way he and other black military personnel were being treated by the United States government, and ultimately the white military generals they answered to. When he and other Tuskegee airmen returned to America after their tours, they didn't receive ticker tape parades. They were nothing like the white soldiers and airmen that they fought with; therefore, they were denied entry into White America's good ole' boy network, which often resulted in access to better educational and vocational opportunities.

But Hancock wasn't one to complain about the inequities in American society. Yes, he thought it was wrong for one group to think it was better than all the others, but an unpublished excerpt from Frederick Douglass's slave narratives opened his eyes to grander possibilities for members of the Black Disapora.

According to Ms. Jackson, this excerpt referenced an encounter that Douglass, Hancock's boyhood hero, had with a green-skinned Satarian named Daygon. Daygon, a human loyalist, took Douglass to his world through something called the Intergalactic Connector. While on Sataria, or the planet contemporary humans call Mars, Douglass was introduced to beings that lived underground but were light years ahead of humanity in the technology department. He also learned from Daygon that the Satarian race was created by Satan for the sole purpose of one day subjugating God's creation, the human race. However, subjugating humanity would not be an easy undertaking, as the Satarian people were known to die within days upon being exposed to the direct descendants of Eden, the black race.

Ms. Jackson said Daygon told Douglass that God created the man Adam in his image from the Garden of Eden's dark sands. God subsequently created the woman Eve from one of Adam's ribs. Because God created the first man and woman from Eden's dark sands, their skin color was black, not white. And because they were first and not last, they received the distinct honor of being called God's chosen people. It should be noted that the Garden of Eden was situated somewhere in the jungles of Africa.

Douglass wrote that Daygon died within hours of their return to Earth due to his extensive exposure to him. But not before Daygon admonished Douglass to write these things down so the direct descendants of Eden would one day read his words, and then strive to understand and fulfill their collective purpose.

The first Adinkrahene Council consisted of Hancock and one African-American representative each from the other three military branches – Army, Navy and Marines. Former NAACP President W.E.B. Dubois served as an advisor to the Council, and played an instrumental role in laying the groundwork for the organization's first reparations management system.

Initially, the RMS was thought to be a legitimate vehicle for recouping what was owed to African Americans past and present. Again, our people had endured 400 years of institutionalized slavery and oppression. It placed a dollar amount on the debt that the United States government owed African Americans. But United States President Franklin D. Roosevelt expressed an unwillingness to distribute cash payments to African Americans. He thought the cash payment measure would be unfair to Americans who were still reeling from The Great Depression. What Hancock and his colleagues didn't know was President Roosevelt was receiving pressure from Corporate Cabal leaders to end his secret negotiations with NAACP leaders.

DuBois ended his relationship with Adinkrahene when Hancock decided to compete with Chicago's Al Capone for control of alcohol sales during the Prohibition era. DuBois still had faith President Roosevelt would come to his senses and make a good faith effort to put African Americans on equal footing with Caucasian Americans. Of course, Hancock knew this would never happen. So, for two years, he siphoned off half a billion dollars from Capone's empire before Capone knew he was being robbed.

When Capone realized he was being played for a sucker by "the blacks," he ordered that Rufus T. Hancock be taken out. Hancock's side business was in banking, so this position made it easier for him to siphon funds from the accounts he managed for Capone. Unfortunately, the golden era of the Adinkrahene Syndicate ended in 1954, when Rufus T. Hancock's bruised, bloodied and mutilated body was found hidden under some trash bags in a Chicago alley.

Adinkrahene faded into the shadows in the years following Hancock's death. But one of Hancock's disciples, 38-year-old Bryson Black, resurrected the organization eleven years later, in 1965. His son Cornelius was eighteen, his daughter Condelezza – or Condi – fifteen. His wife was blues songstress India Mason

Black, who wooed black audiences during performances at New York's Cotton Club and Apollo Theater during the 1950s.

Like Hancock, Bryson wanted to hear apologies from sitting United States presidents, as well as the state governors whose economies were built on the backs of African Americans. He also wanted them to pay these same African Americans for their uncompensated labor and that of their deceased ancestors. Because he knew the wait time would be long and drawn out, he and the three other Council members at the time decided to introduce cocaine, and more potent brands of marijuana, into American markets.

Bryson purchased his supplies from the Mexican Drug Cartel, and made his product available to gang leaders in Los Angeles, Chicago, Detroit, Dallas, Boston and New York. Americans of all hues would purchase these drugs from street dealers. But the unintended consequence was the adverse impact their activities had on members of the Black Diaspora. A disproportionate amount of these members became users and peddlers. And if and when the peddlers got caught by the authorities, they were the first to be arrested, prosecuted, convicted and incarcerated. The Corporate Cabal seemingly perpetuated this inequitable treatment because they thought white lives were more precious than minority ones. Modern-day thought leaders like Michelle Alexander called the mass incarceration of African Americans the New Jim Crow.

Bryson Black went on a killing spree in 1968 after learning that Martin Luther King, Jr. had been assassinated. He loved Dr. King, making a point to always be in the house when Dr. King spoke at one of the New York churches. He had also encouraged Cornelius and Condi to be mindful of Dr. King's words. "He has given us the blueprint for a more equitable America," he once told them.

The NYPD thought they had a serial killer on their hands because the perpetrator had used a knife to carve MLK on his victims' foreheads. When all of the forensic evidence pointed to Bryson Black, the NYPD moved in to arrest him at his Long Island-based dry cleaning business. But rather than allow himself to be arrested, Bryson retreated to a back room to retrieve his military-grade machine gun. Multiple squad cars had come to screeching halts in front of the building, and officers stood outside with their pistols drawn. Bryson opened fire, pelting the officers with a barrage of bullets. Bryson Black was ultimately shot dead that day, but not before he took three NYPD officers with him.

Herbert Newsom inherited the Adinkrahene mantel two years later, vowing to fulfill the organization's mandate using methods rooted in strategy and science. He led the Adinkrahene Reparations Management Syndicate for 23 years. In 1991, he handed the Adinkrahene reins to his protégé Cornelius Black. Cornelius was 45. A year later, Newsom became an Illinois senator. After only one four-year term, he decided to take his skill sets to Washington, DC, where he served three terms in the United States Senate.

"Thank you for your time, Ms. Jackson," I said as I joined Mr. Black in front of the elevator.

"No problem, Jonathan. Just remember, my door is always open. If you have questions, or just need information, don't hesitate to stop by."

"I will. Take care."

The elevator doors slid open, and we exited. We then entered a gymnasium replete with a regulation-sized basketball court. On the far court, six Adinkrahene brothers played a friendly three-on-three basketball game. The other half was occupied by several sitting Adinkrahene brothers and sisters dressed in matching Dri-Fit shorts, shirts and sneakers. Small Adinkrahene symbols were prominently displayed on the front of their shirts. Two other similarly dressed agents with head gear sparred in the center of the mat.

I watched as one of the sparring agents, a female adorned with head gear, jumped high into the air to kick a similarly dressed agent in the chest. The other agent, a large male, flew backwards, bouncing at least two feet across the mat.

The gymnasium erupted with jeers and cheers.

The female agent removed her head gear as her dispatched foe sat upright on the mat. When she turned toward Mr. Black and me, I was pleased to see Selina.

"You ready for this, J?" she asked.

All eyes turned to me.

"Question is," I replied, "are you ready for me?"

I assumed a sparring stance – my feet spread wide, hands inches from my face. I then heard chuckles from the crowd of Adinkrahene agents. Selina could do no more than shake her head and smile.

CHAPTER 4
Kyle Shuler

Atlanta, Georgia is, and always will be, the New South's crown jewel. It serves as an incubator for our free enterprise system. Yes, New York, Boston and Los Angeles receive more accolades, but who cares. Everyone knows the wielders of true economic power reside in Atlanta.

I sat on the sofa reading the *Atlanta Journal-Constitution.* It was late-afternoon, so the housekeeping staff had already cleaned my room and drawn the drapes. Like my other stays in this same room at the Ritz-Carlton Atlanta, I had a clear view of the building that housed CNN's corporate offices. I would be sitting down with the network's Piers Morgan later in the day for my first interview since announcing my presidential bid.

I placed the newspaper on the coffee table, and then walked over to the window. Down in the streets, I could see them, the protesters, trying to put Wall Street on notice. At the time, I wondered if they realized members of the World Trade Organization were meeting in Atlanta to draft proposals that would help them pay their bills? Many of these proposals even had President Newsom's support.

I couldn't see their faces from those lofty heights. My room was on the hotel's seventeenth floor. What I did know is they were mad as hell, thinking we capitalists are the problem rather than the solution. To them, we're nothing more than greedy sons of bitches. I concede that I was greedy. Hell, as the son of a multi-billionaire, I was born with a silver spoon in my mouth. But my mother was more saint than bitch.

The cell phone on my hip vibrated.

"It's time," I said to Roscoe. He was at the wet bar, sipping at another glass of Rum and Coke.

We walked down the room's back hallway toward a large mirror framed in gold. As we approached the mirror, our reflections staring back at us, the wall slid up and away. We stepped into the secret elevator for the short ride to the hotel's sublevel, ten stories below the basement.

Since checking into the hotel, Roscoe and I had barely said two words to each other. As the elevator descended, the only sounds that could be heard were the elevator's humming and ringing, and the rapid beating of my heart. I peeked at the domed camera in the upper right corner of the elevator. The North American-based members of the Cabal's Inner Circle had probably been watching us from the moment our private jet touched down at Atlanta's Hartsfield International Airport.

On the flight over from Washington, Roscoe and I had said about all we could say about the nigras' vendetta against us. Before we left the office, my Mississippi Campaign Manager Claude McDaniel, a nigra himself, called me back to let me know the symbol on the card was definitely an African one. Claude told me to send him one of the cards, and he would have a buddy of his who works for the FBI analyze it. But I brushed his offer off. Even though Claude had been loyal to me for over twenty years, I questioned whether this loyalty would continue if he knew I had slit a darky's throat.

But what would we do without the Boule', the secret society of wealthy nigras who work with even wealthier Whites to sustain Cabal rule? I have no doubt that the Cabal would still exist. We would just have to find another group to exploit, the Mexicans or the Japs perhaps. All I know is George

Washington's plan for controlling the nigras was a complete success. He knew even then that as long as the field nigras envied the house nigras, and we wealthy Whites handsomely rewarded the house nigras for their dedicated service, we would never lose our power and influence over them. At the end of the day, he knew they would jump at the chance to put a few extra bucks in their pockets. Fortunately for us wealthy Whites, these accommodations were enough to appease these house nigras. They were able to achieve a semblance of affluence off our scraps.

There was a time when I questioned this practice. I would rather see these scraps fall into the hands of poor Whites. But that would have caused more nigras to side with Douglass and those traitors to the white race, the Abolitionists. We thought that nigra King was going to get more nigras to support Cabal Rule, but he betrayed us by talking about white leaders writing checks with insufficient funds, and black boys and black girls walking hand-in-hand with white boys and white girls. My father said that's why the order to take him out was given. If his dream became real, it would have taken the Cabal years to regain mental control over the nigras.

The elevator doors slid open, and we stepped into a hallway with walls made of stone and mortar. I could see them, the High Lords, sitting in a semi-circle in the foreground in a hollowed-out chamber. The intermittent drips of echoing water caused a lump to form in my throat.

Even though their faces were completely covered with decorative masks, I knew the High Lord sitting in the middle of the group, in the highest chair, wearing the white mask, was my father. To his left and right sat two other masked lords. Each mask had a monogrammed letter on it – my father A, the others N, G, L and O.

These white gentlemen weren't the richest on the planet, or in America for that matter, but two of them had a tremendous amount of influence over the three branches of federal government – Executive, Legislative and Judicial – while the other three over their state and local cousins.

Roscoe and I took a seat on the stone bench at the center of the semi-circle. They took their time acknowledging us, so we just sat there, listening.

"Newsom's presidency is a threat to Cabal Rule in America, Asia and Europe," High Lord O asserted. "If we don't order the hit, his appeal among Democrats and Independents – and some moderate Republicans – is going to grow."

My father interjected. "It would be foolish of us to elevate the first nigra president to martyr status, my friend."

High Lord N replied, "Lord A is right. If we want to take him out, I suggest we do it once he's out of office. Less influence. Easier target."

"But why wait?" High Lord O continued. "I would much rather pit our champion against a much weaker candidate." He wiped at his covered nose. "A majority of the Blacks, and Hispanics, are going to vote for Newsom, not because he has improved the economy, but because they think he's fighting for them, the middle class."

My father said, "Our operatives in Washington, as well as on Wall Street, know appearances are everything. We own the House, the Democrats the Senate. By refusing to compromise with the Democrats, we have created confusion in Washington. That is adversely affecting domestic and international markets. Herbert Newsom will be out of our hair soon."

High Lord L. "But not if he's reelected. Let's not forget that most Americans are siding with him. Voters blame the GOP for standing in the way of real progress. I say we take him out now."

My father finally acknowledged Roscoe and me. "That won't be necessary, my friend. Senator Shuler here will castrate that nigra with his words." A slight moment of consideration.

"Senator McShane lost the 2008 presidential election to Newsom in a landslide. Senator Shuler's campaign is going to focus on a thriving elite class, how it is better equipped to create private sector jobs."

"We need to craft a different message, if you ask me," High Lord L interrupted. "We lost in 2004 because too many of our corporate executives hoarded their record profits rather than use them to create more private sector jobs. The people are being awakened to the rich getting richer, the poor poorer. Talk of achieving the American Dream now leaves a bad taste in their mouths."

"What do you suggest then, my Lord," my father asked. "That we follow through with Newsom's proposal to take money from our rich brothers and sisters, give it to the poor? To redistribute this country's wealth?"

"It's something we must consider. There will be a high price to pay at the polls if we don't."

"And what do you think that high price will be?" High Lord O asked.

"More lost elections."

"Our man will be elected next November, my brothers. High Lord G has already given us assurances that the Supreme Court will rule in our favor. We just need to make sure our conservative-leaning donors fund targeted campaigns at a higher rate than their liberal counterparts. If they don't, we're screwed."

"Reclaiming the presidency is the top priority here," High Lord G said, "but we must also set our sights on key governorships. Too many wetbacks coming out of the woodworks for us to win elections strictly on the merits of our positions."

As I sat there listening to this back and forth, I found myself admiring High Lord G more than the others. I didn't know who he was, but I knew he had Supreme Court Justice Tobias Bork's ear.

Justice Bork knew that the court's decision in *Citizens United vs. Federal Election Commission* changed the face of American politics. Individual and corporate donors were now allowed to contribute unlimited amounts of money to political campaigns without having to share their identities with the IRS. This anonymity coupled with minimal restrictions would work in our favor. As a result, the Corporate Cabal had high hopes that we Makers would once again be in positions to whip the Takers in line with our conservative ideas. No more free stuff.

"Hello, Senator Shuler," my father greeted. "Mr. Baker."

"Greetings, High Lord," I replied, jumping to my feet out of respect. "Lords."

Roscoe stood as well after I looked over at him. The smirk on his face let me know he found humor in five, professional white men wearing masks. But I let his behavior go because I knew he was still buzzing from the rum and Coke.

My father continued, "So, the nigras 'Civil Rights Movement' has gotten its second wind." His eyes rolled from me to the other High Lords and then back to me.

High Lord O responded, "I thought we silenced their voices in '68 when our man took King out."

"It appears their testicles have grown back," High Lord N quipped.

"This time is different, brothers," my father said. "More personal." He stared down at me. "Their aim is to remove our King from the Chess board." He extended his hand to me. "Senator Kyle Shuler. The next president of these here United States."

I smiled, my eyes moving from Roscoe to the High Lords.

"Yes, sir," I replied.

A sly smile appeared on my father's face. "And you have the Giles girl looking into that other matter for us, Senator Shuler?"

"Yes, sir," I replied.

"Selina?" High Lord G blurted out. "Her investigation won't turn up anything. This group is already raising havoc in our prisons. Our moles in the jails and prisons are telling a different story. Say the niggers there are becoming more confident, more calculating, like they're preparing for some big undertaking. More of them are reading that black inventor's book, uh, *Opportunity Knocks: A Blueprint for Fulfilling Black Dreams.* I couldn't tell you what it's about, but I'm sure the niggers sending us these cards are in cahoots with him."

"Then that joke about their testicles growing back is pure nonsense," High Lord N said. "Their testicles were never severed from their bodies." He breathes in deeply under his mask. "They just sustained deep cuts."

My father responded, "But we all agreed in '82, when Reagan was in office, that declaring a War on Drugs was the right thing to do. At the time, we thought it would allow us to keep the nigras in check without publicly being accused of bigotry and racism."

"But the pressure from Civil Rights groups is mounting, my Lord," High Lord G responded.

"And Newsom appointed a Black to head up the Department of Justice," High Lord O added. He sighs under his mask. "We're losing."

"No!" I interjected, perhaps with too much enthusiasm. All eyes were now on me. "We're going to win this election, and ultimately this fight."

"What other options do we have?" High Lord O asked.

The echoing of footfalls from the long, unlit hallway to my right, the High Lords' left. We all turned to greet our visitor, but all we could see at first were two, pulsating, red lights moving toward us from the darkness.

"Options?" a male voice exclaimed from the cover of darkness. The man finally emerged from the darkness to step into the light. It was Horace, my nephew in public, my son in private. Two ten-foot robots with tentacle-like arms hovered on his left and right flanks.

He continued. "There are plenty of options at our disposal, but only one that makes sense. If the Cabal hopes to maintain its influence and control over the masses, we must employ tactics used by our dear brother Adolf." He paused to nod at his grandfather, High Lord A. My father acknowledged Horace by clasping his hands together and extending them to him. "Our soon-to-be-elected leader - my father Kyle Shuler - and the Republican governors, must rule with iron fists. These nigras, wetbacks and chinks are consuming too much of our resources and wealth. I propose the deployment of our robot army – Combots – right after my father takes the oath of office. Trust me when I say he's going to need the extra protection."

"What can they do?" High Lord O asked.

A wide grin appeared on Horace's face.

"More than you can think or imagine."

Cornelius Black is one of the richest men on the planet for a reason. During my time with the *Post*, I learned that this brother had boldly announced the establishment of Urban Empowerment Zones in the nation's largest cities - Washington, New York, Chicago, Dallas, Atlanta and Los Angeles. He was clearly on a mission to create a new paradigm for black academic achievement and vocational excellence.

"Our first leadership academy was built in 1992," Mr. Black explained, "when Bill Clinton was in office." We were in his spacious office at Holodeck Systems, standing in front of the clear plexiglass window that provided a panoramic view of the District of Columbia's historical sites. "Right here in the DC/ Baltimore area. I had a lot of haters back then. They thought building private charter schools for disadvantaged, black kids was a waste of money. We proved them wrong. One hundred percent of our students graduate in four years to attend the colleges of their choice."

"Who were the people doubting you?" I asked. I sipped from the water bottle that Raquel, Mr. Black's African-American secretary, had given me within minutes of my arrival.

"Other black leaders mostly. Said what I was proposing to do had already been done. Expect another dismal failure, they warned. Said too many of our black kids lack parental support."

"Is the parental support there now?"

"It is. But not at the level I would like. About sixty percent of our parents have bought into our philosophy. I won't be satisfied until we're at one hundred percent."

"I would love to visit one of your schools."

Mr. Black's eyes lit up. "Let's do it now. It's still early in the day. Just a short helicopter ride over the Potomac." As he turned and walked over to his mahogany desk, he cleared his throat with a grunt. "The engineers here at Holodeck have created some pretty amazing things, Jonathan. But the one thing I'm most proud of is the Black Foundation's leadership academies. Mark my word. In twenty years, the American power structure is going to change. And our graduates will be at the forefront."

This was my first time in a helicopter, so when it rose from the Holodeck Systems' rooftop, my stomach dropped and a lump formed in my throat. Mr. Black sat next to me in the back, the African-American pilot and copilot the front.

The pilot allowed the craft to ascend vertically at first, until it was about one hundred yards away from the solar panel-encased building below. The pilot then steered it toward the Washington Monument, which loomed like a lone giant on the horizon. I know Mr. Black saw it, how I had grown more somber and subdued, but I ignored him. I was milking this moment for all its worth, for I was finally getting a birds-eye view of the city I now called home.

After landing on the rooftop of Mr. Black's Baltimore-based Hamilton Sinclair Academy of Excellence, we stepped onto an elevator that took us to the ground floor. When the elevator door opened, and we stepped out of it, we were greeted by smiling African-American fourth and fifth grade students. Should have known Mr. Black would instruct Raquel to call the school administrator so we could be greeted properly. The children were dressed in their formal school uniforms - shirt, tie, slacks and black shoes for the boys, blouses and skirts for the girls. I smiled at all of them, even reaching down to touch the top of one little girl's head in passing.

"Welcome to Sinclair Academy, Mr. Fraiser," a boy standing next to her said.

"Thank you, kind sir," I replied, giving him a fist bump and then watching him walk away with a smile on his face. I then watched the children shuffle to their predetermined marks as Iris Banks, the Head of School, emerged from the front office.

Mr. Black introduced us. I took stock of Iris' athletic physique as I shook her outstretched hand. She reminded me of Selina - tall, dark and lovely. I got an even better look at her hind parts when she leaned in to embrace Mr. Black. Childish oohs and aahs could be heard all around us. I chuckled. But I couldn't help but wonder if Iris also happened to be one of Mr. Black's Adinkrahene agents.

The African and African-American teachers standing near the lobby's sidelines summoned their students to them, where they were then taken back to their respective classrooms. After the lobby had been cleared, Iris asked, "Shall we begin?"

As we walked down long hallways past classrooms full of energetic black children, the empty computer lab and auditorium, Iris recounted the school's beginnings.

The grounds that the school sat on where once home to the Hamilton Sinclair Housing Projects. Hamilton Sinclair was an African-American grocery store owner who lent his time, talent and treasure to revitalizing Washington's east side. A number of influential African Americans once lived in the single-family dwellings surrounding the Sinclair projects during the 1950s and '60s, These homes had long since been abandoned, with their former occupants taking their hopes and dreams to the Northeast or the Midwest, where automotive jobs were plentiful. But who could blame them. Washington's east side had a reputation for being a safe haven for pimps, prostitutes, drug dealers and thieves. When these four groups came together, you adversely changed neighborhood dynamics. Excellence had now been replaced with mediocrity and failure.

Mr. Black decided to invest in Washington's east side first because outsiders jokingly referred to it as Death City. Members of the Grand Ole' Party, or GOP, also made disparaging remarks about the predominantly black neighborhood, and the people who resided there, touting it as a dim reminder of what's wrong in America. Mr. Black retold the story that he told me earlier, how other conservative-minded black leaders inside and outside Washington discouraged him from investing in the community. But Mr. Black essentially told them to go fuck themselves. He wasn't about to give up on the Black Diaspora's future. The stakes were too high.

We stood at the entrance of Sinclair Academy's high school wing. "The students here are the ones that bring me the most joy," Iris exclaimed. She took a few swipes at her eyes, her made-up face, in an attempt to suppress tears. "In the twenty years that this school has been in existence, one hundred percent of them have earned their high school diplomas. You will find many of our graduates at Harvard, MIT, Brown and Stanford. Others at Morehouse, Spelman and Howard."

Mr. Black and I followed Iris through the doors of the library and technology center. The heads of about thirty of the school's seniors turned as they stood to watch us walk over to them. Twenty-five-year-old Virgil Cobb greeted us at the door.

Mr. Cobb, who taught English Language Arts and African-American Literature, extended his hand to Mr. Black first. "Great seeing you again, sir," he exclaimed, excitement and sincere admiration in his voice.

"The feeling is mutual, Mr. Cobb," Mr. Black replied. He then turned to me. "This here is…"

"...J.A. Fraiser," an overweight boy wearing thick lensed glasses interjected a few feet away from us. "He writes for the *Post*. I read his *Culturally Coded* column every Sunday."

Mr. Cobb waved the boy to our group. "I'm Willie," he announced before Mr. Cobb could do the honors. He then reached over to vigorously shake my hand. "Willie Moore. I write too. Working on a novel."

Groans from two girls standing to our left. Iris gave them the look, and they settled down. But it was obvious Willie was the class nerd just because he knew stuff no one else knew.

I released his hand. "I'm sure it will make you a rich man. Let me know when it's available for purchase. I love supporting emerging authors. Know how hard it is getting that first book published." I peered over at the two girls, and then back at Willie. "And let me know if you need something to do this summer. The *Post* offers paid internships to high school students."

Willie looked over at the two girls, a smug expression on his dark face. The girl's mouths dropped as Willie passed them on his way back to his seat. I covered my smile with my hand. Mr. Black bumped my shoulder on the sly while shaking his head.

I then patted Mr. Cobb on his shoulder, giving him a knowing glance. Mr. Cobb nodded his head. He agreed that Bookworm Willie was destined for greatness.

Iris instructed the students to take their seats for the Q & A session.

After everyone was seated, Mr. Black goaded me into asking the first question. I did, saying, "How has your attendance here paved the way for your future success?"

A young lady to my right raised her hand.

"I'll be attending Cornel University in the Fall," she replied. "I want to be a doctor, so I'll major in Biology and then do my residency at Johns Hopkins."

"But you didn't answer my question." I crossed my arms. "How has your attendance here paved the way for future success?"

The young lady's head dropped in embarrassment. Then, she said, "By teaching me how to be a more disciplined student. When I first came here as a sophomore, I felt I was doing good when I made C's. But Mr. Cobb kept telling us that C grades weren't good enough. They're equivalent to F grades." She smiled at Iris. "And having a strong leader like Ms. Banks here is what motivates me to be better than who I am. She's an inspiration to us all. Especially us girls." A wave of nods from the other students. "I want to carry a briefcase like she does. Earn the big bucks."

A few chuckles from the other students.

Mr. Black pointed at a boy seated to his right. "What about you, son? How has your attendance here paved the way for future success?"

The boy stood. "By reminding me that I do have a future if I make the right decisions. Making the right decisions used to be hard for me. My mom needed money, so I started slinging dope to help her out. Never thought I'd get caught, but I did. Spent six months in juvey before Mr. Cobb came to the community center to teach his Prosperity 101 class. Helped me get my priorities straight."

"And why is that so important to you?" I asked.

"Because there are so many opportunities out there for us to take advantage of. I never recognized them because I bought into this notion that being a thug was better than being a scholar. I was wrong. I want a degree. I want a wife, kids. But more than anything, I want to be an agent of change, someone who works with like-minded people to make the world a better place for everyone, not just black people."

"What's your name?"

"Jacob, sir. Jacob Wilson."

"What school will you attend in the Fall?"

"Howard, sir."

"You ready," Mr. Black asked. His hand was on Jacob's shoulder, the other in his pocket.

"As ready as I'll ever be. This is for my Ma. She sees the change in me. And I her. I just want to make her proud, not cause her more pain and grief."

The Washington Post presents
Culturally Coded
A Weekly Column by J.A. Fraiser

NOTHING WORSE THAN AN ANGRY, BLACK...BOY

Enlightened Americans must bring their unenlightened brothers and sisters to the table of justice, equality and fairness. Again, unenlightened Americans are unenlightened because their white members want to blame the victim (i.e., African Americans) rather than take responsibility for their actions and their ancestors' actions. They go through life justifying the subjugation of African Americans, and other persons of color, because they truly believe white people were selected by God to lead the masses. What they don't know is black boys are the ones in the driver's seat. More of them are beginning to understand the scoring system, and this newfound enlightenment is encouraging more of them to use their pent-up anger to diffuse the hold that the Corporate Sector has on unenlightened Whites and complacent Blacks. More importantly, though, the plight of black boys is causing even these unenlightened and complacent members of our society to develop moral compasses.

But are black boys angry? I tend to think so. But why? Well, for starters, America has a long history of designating them as Enemies of the State. I have already provided evidence of this maltreatment in my previous columns, most notably those about the senseless death of teenager Trayvon Martin. But we must also be cognizant of the full court press that the Corporate Sector's acolytes are applying to black boys in their homes, schools and communities.

We can argue all day about the need for African Americans in general to take responsibility for their lives. Taking responsibility means they will make the kind of decisions that help promote true upward mobility. But when you have a majority of our black boys growing up in homes devoid of dominant male role models, you have to ask yourself why. Is it something African Americans are doing to themselves? Or is it part of a long-standing conspiracy to keep African Americans in a subservient position?

It's probably a mix of both extremes. I say this because it all goes back to decisions, the values that African Americans hold dear. African Americans know that their families are in a state of disarray because a majority of their black men aren't standing in the gap for their women and children, or they committed a crime that prevents them from standing anywhere near their women and children. The former is inexcusable. Why would grown-ass men - in their right minds, mind you - allow their children to fend for themselves? However, the latter is preventable.

There are a lot of black fathers out there who have it all wrong. They think being a man equates to sleeping with any woman who is able and willing. Because so many of our black men harbor such thoughts, we have black children who were, and are, born out of wedlock. And we know what that means. It means these children will grow up not ever knowing their biological fathers, whose selfishness seems quite despicable because their hearts and minds are focused on one thing - literally sticking it to the women in their lives.

The mass incarceration of black men should not be attributed solely to black men. Yes, one has to decide if he wants to be a criminal, but the Corporate Sector knowingly creates conditions that support the demonization of black boys and men. In our public schools, teachers of all hues feel threatened the most by black boys. Consequently, these same teachers take control of their fears by removing black boys from their classrooms under the guise of in-school or out-of-school suspensions. These teachers tell us they don't have time for belligerent black boys. They want to spend more time working with their cooperative students, the ones that show through their words and deeds that they want to learn.

What these teachers fail to understand is they are black boys only defense against criminality. We all know that children under the age of 16 are required to attend school five days a week. But when teachers give up on large segments of their student bodies, they are essentially issuing jail and/or death sentences. Without responsible and competent teachers to help them identify their skill sets, they gravitate to what I refer to as the Knuckleheads, teenagers and young adults who live for today rather than deliberately plan for tomorrow.

But the Corporate Sector has also succeeded in relegating black boys and their families to dying communities. Cities like Detroit and Cleveland were once thriving with leisure activities and employment opportunities for all. But decades later, one has declared bankruptcy while the other is trying to reclaim its identity.

Like I said in my previous columns, there are Caucasian Americans out there that share my concerns about black boys. My hope is they will shake themselves free of the Corporate Sector's influence and control to support activist Blacks' quest to save our native sons. Standing on the sideline and saying, "I don't give a damn about those people," isn't going to cut it in this day and age. I also hope they will get on board with President Herbert Newsom's *My Brother's Keeper* Initiative. This initiative seeks to reverse under-achievement among young black and Hispanic males. If and when this happens, black boys, and black men, will become a little less angry.

CHAPTER 6
Jonathan Fraiser

I scooted to the edge of the sofa to snatch my ringing smart-phone from the end table.

"Yo, dude." It was Tyler Smith, my old accountability partner from Living Water Community Church. I hadn't seen or heard from him since my separation and divorce from Carmelita. "Where you been?"

"Around," I mumbled.

"The brothers at church keep asking about you. Told them I'd give you a call."

It was right then and there that I regretted taking a harsh tone with Tyler. Even though he was a white dude, I had no qualms with him. It also helped that his wife Mary was black, and that he taught English at Douglass, one of the district's toughest public high schools. Situated in an urban area, over eighty percent of its students were black. Tyler often invited me to speak to his students about my work with the *Post*.

The one time that I did share with his students, during one of their career days, I found myself staring into a sea of blank faces. But their demeanors changed when I started dropping the names of powerful politicians. I was amazed at how much they knew about these public figures, but, more importantly, current events.

Tyler and I arrived in Washington on the same day back in 2000. We actually sat next to each other in coach on an American Airlines flight from Knoxville, Tennessee. I wanted to sleep. Tyler wanted to talk. When our flight landed at Washington's Dulles Airport, we exchanged numbers, not knowing we would see each other a few weeks later, with our spouses, at Living Water.

"I appreciate that, Tyler, man," I replied, leaning back a little on the sofa, phone secured between my shoulder and ear. But I felt myself clamping down on my bottom lip. I didn't know what to say next. What was I going to tell him? I joined a group that is committed to bringing people who looked like him to justice? I don't think so.

"How are things down at Douglass?" I asked.

"Couldn't be better. Principal resigned. They hired me to replace him."

"That's great, man. Julia still writing?"

Julia was his 15-year-old, bi-racial daughter. She was also one of the students present during my last visit to the school. "She's editor of the school paper. May be joining you one day, down at the *Post*."

I scratched my right thigh with my free hand. "If that's what she wants to do, more power to her."

"Mary and I saw Carmelita at the grocery store the other day. Appeared to be happy. Hard seeing her with another man, though."

"She deserves to be happy after what I put her through."

A slight pause, then, "What about you, Jonathan? You happy?"

"I am. My book is selling. Been on all the major talk shows. And I have just been nominated for the Pulitzer Prize. Can't get much better than that."

"What about your spiritual life? The last time we spoke, you were talking about moving back down south, to Atlanta."

"Decided to stay."

A much longer pause.

"We should get together sometime, for lunch. Catch up."

I knew what "catch up" meant. It meant he wanted to back me in a corner so he could hear all about my many sins. I really didn't have the stomach for that. I had grown content with my sinful ways. Truth be told, I wasn't a bad person, at least by my standards. I just had a weakness for beautiful women.

The facility that existed under Mr. Black's mansion was impressive, but that was nothing compared to what existed on the outskirts, about 100 miles west, under the Shenandoah Mountain range. Over the years, Mr. Black and the four members of Adinkrahene's Leadership Council had overseen the development of The Cradle, a top-secret, underground compound where agents would come to train for missions and receive intelligence briefings about Jim Crow criminals.

Agents had to board and ride a shuttle to get from the surface to the underground facility. This shuttle was unlike anything I had ever seen, because it cleaved through dirt and rock by warping the space around it. No one knows what kind of experiments the founders conducted to develop the Slipstream technology, but Big Nate and I hoped the answer awaited us at The Cradle.

A much older brother, who was already on the shuttle when Big Nate and I got on, sat near the far wall reading something on his tablet computer. It became obvious this shuttle made multiple stops. I also got the impression the older brother was one of Adinkrahene's more experienced agents.

"Where you from?" I asked Big Nate. He was the agent that Selina kicked to the mat during my first visit to the mansion.

"Atlanta," he replied. "You?"

"Washington."

The older brother looked over at us.

"Detroit," he exclaimed, with a wide grin on his face.

"Is any of this making any sense to you guys?" I shrugged my shoulders. "I didn't think black folks did this kind of stuff. This kind of stuff only happens in Octavia Butler novels, right?"

"It was kind of strange to me too," Big Nate said. "Holograms that look like real people. Bit much if you ask me."

The older brother. "Don't worry, you'll get used to it. Cornelius brought you here to be amazed."

"What's your name?"

The older brother stood up and walked over to where we were sitting. "Name's Otis," he exclaimed, extending his hand to me while placing his tablet on the coffee table. I shook his hand. "Otis Wilson. But most of the agents just call me Doc." I watched as Doc shook Big Nate's hand and then sat a few feet down from me on the sofa.

"How long you been here?" Big Nate asked Doc.

"Since the beginning. Traveling to The Cradle to perform a few upgrades."

"Upgrade? You a computer technician or something?" I interjected.

Doc smiled. "I know. Too much information, right? But you traveling to The Cradle on one of our Slipstream Shuttles, or what Cornelius calls our A trains, means he's about to grant you access to all of our secrets."

"What kind of secrets?" Big Nate asked, leaning forward.

Doc looked us over before continuing. "You ever wonder what it's like to achieve a higher level of existence."

Big Nate and I exchanged glances before shaking our heads no.

"You learned in your training at the mansion that Jatube is an ancient African fighting style that allows us to tap into our Ta-Roo, or force of will."

Doc's tablet rose from the table to hover in front of us. My eyes were the first to widen.

"It is what allows us to store up power in our cores." Doc patted his stomach. His floating tablet simultaneously rose a little higher and then began circling over our heads. "We release this power when we attack our opponent, or block his attacks." The tablet floated back to its original position, and then slowly descended to the coffee table. "We have created technology that will give us the power to strike fear into the hearts of our enemies."

"But who are our enemies," Big Nate asked. "The Corporate Cabal..."

"Or white people," I interjected.

Doc replied, "Not all white people are bad, Jonathan. Just the unenlightened ones. We just need to convince more of them to work with us, not against us."

I said, "All of this has to be about more than that, Doc."

"It is. The Corporate Cabal is controlled by White Anglo-Saxon Protestant males. That fact is indisputable. But these unenlightened Whites, and complacent Blacks, make life more difficult for us activist Blacks. Both groups enrich themselves off the black underclass's poverty. We call these complacent Blacks the Boule'. Therefore, our number one objective as Adinkrahene agents is to teach our young black boys and black girls how to embrace prosperity without bowing at the thrones of white supremacy and corporate greed. They need to see with their own eyes what powerful and incorruptible black people can do with their collective force of will. "

Big Nate asked, "So, Mr. Black wants to show that black people are the superior race?"

"No. Not at all. Cornelius wants us to work with like-minded African-Americans and Africans to right the White majority's wrongs, make them do right by black people, and other persons of color. You see, the legitimate exertion of our power usually goes unnoticed by our black children, unless we're performing on the stage, in film or on a playing field. That's what the

Corporate Cabal wants them to see." Doc stood as the A Train came to a stop. Big Nate and I followed his lead as the shuttle door hissed open. "I'm Adinkrahene's chief neurosurgeon. Cornelius and I developed the Slipstream Interface more than ten years ago. He offered me an opportunity to change the world, and I jumped at it. Humanity must learn to get along, brothers. A kingdom divided cannot stand."

Big Nate and I followed Doc off the A Train and onto the landing platform. We were in a cavern, with stalagmites hanging from the ceiling, stalactites jutting up from the ground. A large, disk shaped, underground facility with windows – The Cradle - was in the foreground. I turned to see Big Nate looking behind the A Train. I could tell he still couldn't believe the A Train flew through the Earth as easily as an airplane flew through the sky.

A bridge extended from the landing platform to the facility's entrance. About fourteen Adinkrahene agents – all African-American and African – stood in two rows of seven facing us, all of them dressed in black. My attention immediately went to Iris. She acknowledged me with a head nod as she and the other agents stood at attention, their hands behind their backs.

Mr. Black approached us from the other side of the bridge.

"Welcome to The Cradle, brothers." Mr. Black extended his hand to me, and I shook it. I then watched him nod at Doc as he shook Big Nate's hand. "I hope the ride down was a pleasant one."

"Yes, sir." I replied. "It was." I swung my arms upwards and outwards. "But you didn't prepare us for this."

Big Nate nodded his head in agreement.

Mr. Black instructed Iris and Agent Jacob Cummings to escort us to our quarters. All of the compound's guest rooms were fully furnished, and included a living room, bedroom, dining area, fitness pod and bathroom. When I opened my window drapes, I found myself peering down at the underground stream that flowed around the pillar of land that The Cradle rested on. The facility lights kept the cavern lit. If not for the cavern walls, I would have never known we were more than fifty miles underground.

Iris said as she watched me from the room's foyer, "When I first got here, I had a panic attack. Claustrophobic. But we're allowed to take one of the A trains to the surface anytime we want."

I turned from the window to her. "How long have you been an agent?"

"Just celebrated three years last week. They recruited me right out of graduate school."

"Where'd you earn your degree"

"Brown University up in Providence, Rhode Island. Majored in Higher Education Administration."

My doorbell chimed. Iris was closer to the door than me, so she did me a solid by opening it.

"Selina!" Iris joyfully exclaimed as Selina entered the room.

"Hey, girl," Selina replied, hugging Iris in passing. "How you been?"

"Great. Just helping Jonathan here get situated."

I smiled.

Standing in my bedroom doorway, Selina turned up her lips, saying, "Be careful around this one. All he wants to do is get in them drawers. Right, J?"

I lied. "Wrong." I then swept Selina off her feet and swung her around. "But I would like to get into yours."

Iris got the message, smiling at us as she showed herself out.

Chapter 7
Selina Giles

"You're out, Selina."

I was in FBI Director Robert Young's office, seated in one of his leather chairs. Director Young glared at me from behind his oversized desk, over piles of paper and active case files.

He continued, "I instructed you to leave it alone. But you went behind my back and reopened it anyway. What were you thinking, girl?"

My head jerked up. I didn't like being called a girl, especially when the comment came from the likes of him, a white man. But Director Young was right. I had discreetly reached into the cookie jar one time too many. Now, any evidence that the FBI had amassed about my grandmother's case would be off-limits to me.

Director Young leaned forward, placing his arms on his desk. "You're suspended, indefinitely. Can't have my agents settling old scores, especially when the person you're trying to settle a score with is trying to become the leader of the free world." He inhaled deeply. "Hand over your badge and firearm."

"You and I both know he did it," I snapped as I stood. I pulled my pistol from my side holster, slamming it on his desk. "He doesn't deserve to be president."

"Your opinion, Selina. Not mine." He watched him flinch when I tossed my badge onto his desk. "Get over it."

His last comment infuriated me, but I didn't want to give him the pleasure of seeing how upset I was. "Can I be excused?"

"Yes."

I stood up and slowly made my way to his office door. But I couldn't resist the urge to stare him down one last time. The stern look on my face let him know that I despised him, what he represented.

At first, he matched my glare. When he looked away like the be-otch I knew he was, I left him. Outside his office, and in the bustling hallway, I smiled, taking a victory lap in my mind. I walked down the long hallway to what would soon be known as my former office, rage bubbling inside me.

Director Young was your typical white man. Typical white men like him are quick to say we Blacks should get over 400 plus years of slavery and Jim Crow legislation, but they never take responsibility for their own actions.

I spotted J sitting on a bench across the street from the FBI Building. He wore a heavy winter coat and matching hat. The sun had finally broken through the clouds, but there still was a chill in the Washington, DC air. J stood when he saw me standing there with my briefcase hanging from my shoulder strap. He greeted me as I walked across the street.

"How'd it go?" he asked, taking my briefcase from me. We both turned to walk to the parking garage.

"Like I expected. They just don't get it, J."

I had told him as much the night before, when he arrived at my Georgetown condominium looking for some loving. We must have spent hours getting each other off that night. He took me to the moon and back, carefully exploring every crevice of my body before going down on me or putting it in. After the loving was over, though, we held each other tight, reminiscing about the past, mentally preparing ourselves for our new lives together as Adinkrahene agents.

"How do you balance the two?" he had asked me as we lay naked on the bed under satin sheets.

"What do you mean?" I had replied.

"Working for the FBI while forcing Jim Crow criminals to account for their crimes."

"By telling myself they're one and the same. As an FBI agent, I have full access to any evidence that has been collected."

"Won't your boss question your motivation for thumbing through evidence, especially evidence pertaining to your grandmother?"

I had flipped to my side to face him. "What he doesn't know won't hurt him. Besides, he doesn't know. Never log my visits to the archives. Just take and copy what I need."

"But I'm sure they have cameras down there. I know we do down at the *Post*, in our archival area. What are you going to say when they catch you?"

"They won't." I had sighed. "I'm good at what I do."

But apparently I wasn't good enough.

We entered a public parking lot, walked past rows upon rows of cars. The plan was to get a bite to eat and then summon the A Train for a Slipstream flight back to The Cradle. But as we walked to the car, I sensed that someone was watching us. When I checked our sixes, though, all I saw was a well-dressed white guy puffing on a cigarette in front of the elevator doors. And to our right was a group of older white women getting out of a car.

J looked me over as he unlocked and opened the passenger side door. I frowned. "What's wrong?"

"Spider sense. Going crazy right now. Feel like somebody's watching us."

J chuckled at my hero reference. He will probably always be a kid at heart. Back in college, he always had his head buried in a Marvel or DC comic book. But I was serious. I guess that's why I instinctively balled up my fist, a clear sign that I was charging my Ta-Roo.

I worried about J, though. He was one of Adinkrahene's newest recruits. He probably could have handled himself in a fist-fight – he scored high marks during his Jatube trials – but he had not been connected to the Slipstream Grid. Moreover, all this talk about black folk bringing Jim Crow criminals to account for their crimes was probably making his head spin. But I was committed to helping him adjust to this new reality.

J didn't know this at the time, but my father intended on using him and his gifts to drive a dagger through the Corporate Cabal's heart. The first book J ever wrote got everyone's attention because it referenced mass incarceration, how it was being used to siphon wealth from black and brown Americans. He identified companies on the New York Stock Exchange and Dow Jones indexes that paid private investors large sums of money for locking ethnic minorities up. When the full weight of what he was reporting hit me, I immediately went to my father to make the case for why J had to be an Adinkrahene agent. Of course, I never thought we would end up being bed buddies. But I'm not one to knock an added bonus.

As J backed his Honda Accord up and shifted to drive, I saw the smoker toss his cigarette aside before ducking into a Suburban that had pulled up to the curb in front of him. I bit my tongue because I didn't want to alarm J. But once he drove the car past the exit gate after paying the parking attendant, I said, "Someone's tailing us."

J's eyes shot to the rearview mirror. The Suburban was already through the gate as he pulled his Accord onto the road.

"Not for long," J replied as we approached an intersection. The light was green, but it turned yellow ten yards out. It was then that J pressed the pedal to the metal to send the car speeding past the light and across the intersection before the light turned red.

I turned, looking through the rearview window. The Suburban's driver was cussing at his colleagues, slapping at the steering wheel. They were now at the mercy of the red light, and the thick traffic on the intersecting street.

Chapter 8
Jonathan Fraiser

After our encounter with the Suburban crew, both Selina and I knew taking her back to Georgetown was a bad idea. Someone viewed her as a threat, and wanted to take her out. Before I could ask her what she wanted to do, the Bluetooth earpiece attached to her right ear flashed green.

She tapped the button on the device to accept the call. I expected her to offer a greeting, but she said nothing. She just listened, shook her head, and then pressed the button again to end the call.

"Drop me off here," she demanded, pointing at a Popeye's Chicken restaurant further down the street on the left side of the street.

"Why here? You about to order a two-piece meal or something?"

"Just do it," she chuckled, slapping my arm.

I swerved my Accord to the curb.

Selina held on to the passenger side door as she prepared to exit. "This is where we part ways, J."

"Why don't you hide out at The Cradle? They'll never find you there."

Selina turned toward the restaurant without offering a response. A bearded brother appeared out of nowhere. He waved her to him from the side of the building. "When they come, have some canned responses. They're going to grill you about our relationship. Tell them the truth. But they're also going to ask you about the symbol. You know nothing. Understand?"

"Yeah. I understand." She then got out of the car. I immediately rolled the window down after she pushed the passenger door shut. "Will I see you again?"

"That's on you." She blew me a kiss as she walked backwards. "Complete your training. You're going to make one helluva agent."

Selina then trotted over to the bearded brother with her briefcase in hand. After she disappeared behind the building, the bearded brother threw me a hand sign, an upside down V, or A, I think. Not knowing how to respond, I just gave him a thumbs-up and drove away.

Three days passed. No visit from the FBI or the CIA. No phone calls from Selina. Maybe they didn't place us together, I thought.

I had requested a three-month sabbatical from the *Post* so I could spend my waking hours training at The Cradle.

Information Technology.

Strategic Planning.

Investigative Techniques.

Political Science.

More Martial Arts.

I learned that some of the agents that had been awarded access to The Cradle were carefully vetted African-American male and female graduates from Historically Black Colleges and Universities, or HBCUs. Most of these graduates had viewed films like Foxy Brown, Superfly and Shaft as kids, and now they were excited about this opportunity to take it to "The Man". But the roster also included reformed black inmates who saw the light in the months leading up to their prison releases. They were carefully vetted as well. I, on the other hand, just wanted to ride this roller coaster to its end.

Exposing Kyle Shuler for what he was - a cold-blooded killer - would put other Jim Crow criminals on notice that their crimes against humanity would not go unpunished.

"You heard from Selina?" I asked Mr. Black one night over dinner.

"She's gone rogue, Jonathan," he replied. The intensity on Mr. Black's face was unsettling. He used his fork to consume more of the sweet potato casserole on his plate. "We're trying to embarrass the bastard, not assassinate him."

"But Selina's no killer."

Mr. Black looked over at me as if to say, Nigger, please!

"Selina has been with us for over fifteen years, Jonathan. Sister-girl has seen some things. Done even worse. One of our best students then, perhaps our best agent now. But she has been doing some underhanded things. Done formed her own band of thieves. Call themselves Black-Out."

After that, I returned to my room. Still had a hard time believing Selina could betray Mr. Black, her Adinkrahene brothers and sisters. She seemed so loyal and committed to the cause. Part of me wanted to empathize with her. Early on, she and I both agreed that Adinkrahene justice was too slow, too calculated. But the worst thing we Adinkrahene agents could do was become cold-blooded killers like the Jim Crow criminals we hunted. So, as I stared down at the underground stream from my bedroom window, I quiet calm washed over me.

Could Selina's belligerence be part of Mr. Black's master plan?

Could it be a precursor to the Adinkrahene Syndicate's heroic acts?

These questions would haunt me until Selina emerged from obscurity.

Chapter 9
Kelli Shuler

Washington's Cedar Creek Country Club was the site of the fundraiser my brother Horace Shuler hosted for Daddy after he announced his bid for the White House. At first, I wasn't going to go. I had a long history of turning heads when I stepped into rooms. The thought of old, decrepit males fawning over me was repulsing. But Daddy's announcement was a major one. As a result, I didn't mind the fawning as long as it motivated these power-brokers to put their hard-earned cash in the basket.

"Baby sis," Horace exclaimed as I exited the house and walked onto the patio. He had been chatting with DC Mayor Lucas Chase. Chase's wife stood by his side with a toothy grin on her face. She wore a shiny, garnet-colored dress, diamond necklace and earrings. Mayor Chase was dressed like all of the other male attendees, black suit and tie.

"Glad you could make it." Horace pulled me in close for a hug, and then released me. "This here is my sister Kelli, Mayor. She just recently started working for our father, as his Communications Director."

"You must be the one feeding Kyle all those scathing talking points about Newsom's Affordable Care Act."

"That would be me," I replied, somewhat sheepishly. Who are these people? I thought.

The mayor's wife interjected. "You must be disheartened by the latest news. Those whackos over on MSNBC claim improvements have been made to the website. More and more people are enrolling each day."

"I heard," I replied. "But we mustn't believe everything we hear, right? Wouldn't be good for House Republicans. You know they have voted over 40 times to repeal it."

Horace said, "But those were important votes, sis. Wouldn't you agree, Mayor?"

"Most definitely," Mayor Chase exclaimed. "We need an enthusiastic conservative base if we hope to win the Presidency, boot the Liberals from the Senate."

I did a quick scan of the people around me, still listening. I spotted Mommy sitting on one of the outdoor sofas with a group of DC socialites. An African-American waiter hovered nearby, ready to refresh the wine in their wine glasses upon request. The other women just sat there listening, half-filled wine glasses dangling from their outstretched hands. Daddy held court toward the back of the patio, near the rail. A mixture of young and old men stood near him, vying for his attention.

My head and eyes shot to the Mayor. "We won't be winning much of anything if we don't expand the tent, make it more inclusive." I turned to direct his attention to the people in the room. "We're an island unto ourselves. I don't see many Blacks here. Mexicans either. Lord knows we're going to need their votes during the 2012 presidential election and the 2014 mid-terms. We can no longer afford to be the white people's party."

As soon as these words were spoken, I spotted Claude McDaniel and his wife Delores standing a few feet away from Gramps. About three more African-American couples, and two Hispanic, were in attendance, but these kinds of numbers would do nothing to enhance our reputation among racial/

ethnic minorities, especially with select members of the press being present. We had to do more, but I didn't know what more could be done. That was until I saw Jonathan exit the house, wine glass in hand, to stand to Daddy's left.

"Excuse me," I said, patting Horace on the sleeve and then waving at the Mayor and his wife. I could feel their eyes scanning the faces of the people in front of me as I walked away.

"Funny seeing you here, Mr. Fraiser," I exclaimed with a hint of sarcasm. "Haven't seen you since Daddy made his announcement."

"Been away on sabbatical," Jonathan replied, "working on another book project." He looked me over, from head to toe. "How you been?"

"Good." One of the waiters walked past us on his way to the kitchen, grazing my backside. The bump caused me to lose my balance, fall into Jonathan's outstretched arms.

Jonathan smiled down at me as he held me upright. "I done told you to lay off the booze," he joked. We both chuckled at that. I spotted Daddy, Horace and others looking in our direction, which prompted me to lead Jonathan off the patio and onto the back lawn, where a platoon of tables and chairs awaited us.

Once seated, Jonathan asked, "How's all this making you feel?"

"That he's going to pull it off." I then paused. I knew Jonathan had voted for Republican lawmakers in the past, but I also knew he listed himself as an Independent during the 2008 Presidential Election, ultimately voting for Newsom and Democratic candidates during the 2010 midterm elections. Consequently, I felt I had to choose my words carefully.

"I need your help," I announced.

"What kind of help? Jonathan replied.

"I...I mean we need you to write something positive about my dad, something that will let African Americans know he's on their side."

"I thought he was. At least that's what he said when he was running for the Senate."

"He is. You know that. But the Shuler name isn't one you associate with African-American progress. But Gramps has done a lot for African Americans. He was against President Reagan's War on Drugs. Everyone knows that piece of legislation is wreaking havoc on poor people, communities of color."

"I do. But nothing ever came of it. Members of his party lambasted the bill. Young, black men are still getting stopped, frisked and arrested at disproportionate levels."

"But if he can withstand ridicule from the right-wing extremists in our party, I'm certain he's willing to up the ante once he becomes president."

The look on Jonathan's face told me that he wasn't buying it. But that was all I had. The truth is that was the only stance Gramps had taken for the Blacks. Moderates like Jonathan, but mostly Progressives, thought Gramps was complicit in the Republican Party's plan to place restrictions on early voting and to eliminate voting on Sundays. The latter had black pastors in an uproar, because immediately after Sunday morning church services, they would lead their congregants to local election offices to get them registered. Once early voting began, they were even allowed to cast their votes on Sundays.

My grandfather and others knew ending this practice would give our candidates a better chance of winning. But the backlash was severe, as the talking heads on MSNBC and CNN said we were declaring war against racial/ethnic minorities, women and college students. They also claimed we were restricting the vote rather than expanding it.

"All I see is a candidate and a party calling poor Blacks and other persons of color Takers. Let's not forget Mayor Chase's forty-seven percent comment."

Jonathan leaned forward in his chair, awaiting my response. But I had no desire to go there with him. What Mayor Chase had said was indefensible, repulsive even.

During a local fundraiser for the Washington, DC Mayor's race, Chase was caught on film telling a group of wealthy donors that there were 47 percent of Americans who would never vote for him, or other Republican lawmakers. He reasoned that they wouldn't vote for him because Democratic lawmakers always promised to give them "stuff" instead of requiring them to be personally responsible for securing "stuff" for themselves. Even I agreed with much of what Mayor Chase had said. That's the basis of Capitalism. But I felt the comment ruined any chance Conservatives had of welcoming African Americans and other racial/ethnic minorities into the Republican Party.

"And I already told you that I have nothing else to say about that. It was wrong. Insensitive even. But my father is not a pea in Mayor Chase's pod. There are plenty of Republicans who disagree with the man. They choose to remain silent because the Establishment supports this kind of talk."

"And there lies the problem," Jonathan said, rapping his fingers across the table. "The RNC endorses the views of some of its most extremist and intolerant candidates. If you ask me - and I know you didn't - that's not a winning strategy."

Jonathan was right. But what else were we going to do? Everyone in the Republican Party had already conceded that Newsom was going to capture much of the Black vote. Our only option was to craft a message that won the hearts and minds of Whites who resented the fact that the federal government gave Blacks free stuff after President Lyndon B. Johnson signed the Civil Rights Act of 1964. But we also needed to capture at least thirty percent of the Hispanic vote to even be competitive in the Presidential race. That's when I decided it was time to change the subject.

"What interest do you have in the FBI?" I asked. I watched Jonathan's once-aggressive demeanor melt away.

"At the press conference," I continued. "I saw you talking with our dear friend Selina Giles." The wrinkles in my brow became more pronounced as I watched Jonathan twist and turn in his chair. "What? You didn't think we would be monitoring who members of the press interact with?"

Jonathan replied, "No. That's not it. I'm just surprised to see the question coming from you. Mr. Baker's usually the one doing the grilling."

"Mr. Baker isn't the only person being paid to make my father look good. To protect his professional and private interests."

"Understood."

I turned to look back toward the patio. A number of the attendees stood on the deck chatting. I spotted my brother reacquainting Mayor Chase and his wife with Daddy.

"Someone has been threatening my father, Jonathan." I placed one of the aluminum cards with circles on the table in front of him. "We don't think Selina's the one making them. She will always have ties to our family, even though none of us have reached out to her directly since she graduated from the FBI Academy in Quantico. Daddy had me send an email invite after Director Young told him she had been reassigned to D.C."

"That's great. That she would reach out to your father, I mean. I know what happened to her grandmother. She told me about it when we were at Tennessee together."

"What did she tell you?"

"That she wouldn't rest until her grandmother's killer was identified, prosecuted and jailed."

"I don't blame her. Pa-Paw adored her. I guess that's why he tried so hard to help her deal with the loss."

Pa-Paw, or Great Granddaddy Watson, had created a special savings account for Selina in the months following Ms. Mary's death. She had access to the account on her eighteenth birthday. It only amounted to a little over two hundred and fifty thousand dollars, but that was more than enough for Selina to purchase her first car, make a down payment on her first home. Pa-Paw even paid for private counseling, and attended her undergraduate graduation ceremony. He told Selina then that he was proud of her, and that her grandmother would have been even prouder.

"No. The times we were together, she had nothing but kind things to say about Mr. Watson, your father and aunt. But I know finding her grandmother's killer is what keeps her awake most nights."

"Were the two of you lovers?"

"No. Just friends. She was dating my teammate. Bank Shot."

"What about now? You interested in getting with her like you got with me."

I could tell my question caught him off guard. He chuckled, looked away, but didn't offer a response.

"You're incorrigible, Jonathan Fraiser."

"I'm a man, Kelli. Hard to resist the allure of beautiful women."

"Well, I'll consider that a compliment. But that let's me know where we stand."

As soon as I mouthed these words, a woman's scream rung out from the patio deck. Jonathan and I looked up to see a female dressed from head to toe in what appeared to be a black, Spandex bodysuit. A Plexiglas faceplate masked her identity. She hovered about twenty feet from Daddy. Daddy's bodyguards rushed over to him with their pistols drawn, daring the woman to take another step.

She extended her arms toward the bodyguards as her faceplate dissolved to give us a clear view of her face. It was Selina, her hair tied back in a ponytail. But then it happened. Selina waving her hand and bodyguards flying through the air and over the patio railing to land a few feet from where Jonathan and I were sitting. Seeing that, Daddy and several of the other guests ran into the house.

Realizing there was no time to corral my father, Selina turned her full attention to me. Jonathan and I watched in amazement as her body rose a little higher and floated toward us.

"We can either do this the easy way," she said as her feet touched down on the manicured lawn, "or the hard way. Your choice."

Jonathan placed himself between Selina and me. "Don't do this, Selina."

Selina chuckled as she crossed her arms and shifted her feet, one in front of the other. "Someone must pay," she replied. She then pressed her fists together, pointed them at Jonathan, and fired some kind of invisible beam into his chest. The blast hit Jonathan dead center, knocking him off his feet and into some rented tables, about thirty feet from where he had been standing.

I tried to rush over to him to make sure he wasn't seriously injured. But before I could reach him, the same invisible force that Selina had used on Jonathan tightened around my arms and torso to lift me off the ground. Seconds later, I found myself flying with her away from the mansion and through the Maryland sky.

CHAPTER 10
Horace Shuler

"What are you doing?" Daddy exclaimed as he pursued me through the nearly empty house. The cleaning crew buzzed around us looking like penguins in an ice chalet, picking up after our long-departed guests. Daddy grabbed my arm, prompting me to stand there, listen to what he had to say. "The plan is to activate them after the election, not before."

I crossed my arms, doing my best to angle my body away from him.

"That's my sister, your daughter, out there, Daddy. I can't just sit here and do nothing. Not when my Combots can give that bitch a dose of her own medicine."

"But that's not part of the plan, Horace. You know that. If I'm going to win this election, we can't afford any slip-ups." He playfully chopped my arm for emphasis. "Besides, you already told me SANDI is close to locking in on her location."

I had dispatched the floating sphere known as SANDI, or Surveillance Android for National Defense and Intelligence, within an hour of Kelli's abduction. But the tracking device that had been surgically implanted into Kelli's right arm years ago, when she had to go under to have her tonsils removed, went cold. More than 30 hours had passed since we lost the signal, and even though I had uploaded all available video and audio to SANDI's rapid access memory bank, we were no closer to locating Kelli.

There was a part of me that felt Selina would never harm Kelli, not after recalling how they interacted with each other during Selina's summer visits to our parents' Mississippi estate. Selina was attending the University of Tennessee at the time. My sister adored Selina, to Daddy and Pa-Paw's chagrin. I even winced at the sight of them. This darkie treated my sister like she was part of her family.

After Mary Giles' murder, Pa-Paw went out of his way to make Selina feel comfortable around us, ultimately opening up a savings account for her at Jackson Federal Bank and Trust. Yes, Daddy had slit her grandmother's throat. And Daddy had no remorse for his actions. He, much like Pa-Paw before him, knew we had to keep the nigras down so the more enlightened members of the Caucasian race could lead.

Both Daddy and Pa-Paw were masters at keeping their friends close, their enemies closer. They didn't have to give Selina anything after she graduated from UT, but they did.

Pa-Paw made the first deposit into the special account that had been opened in Selina's name. I believe it was about fifty thousand dollars. This deposit gave Daddy, who was a teen-ager at the time, the time he needed to work with my mother to concoct a believable story regarding my birth. Shame would have been heaped upon our family if the public knew Daddy had impregnated his adopted sister. He also managed to grad-uate from Ole' Miss with an undergraduate degree in Political Science, and from Harvard University with a graduate degree in Corporate Law.

With two degrees in hand, and the bar examination behind him, he secured full-time employment with a New York law firm. When the money started rolling in from his day job, he added another two hundred thousand dollars to Selina's bank account.

My grandfather didn't mince words when he told Daddy that he would need Selina's loyalty and support. He had already predicted that my father would one day become the next Shuler Republican. Therefore, he was the first to feel compelled to win Selina and her family over, showering them with gifts and money. He wanted to shield our family from any accusations that a member of his family had anything to do with Mary Giles' murder.

I pulled the patio door inward and then stepped outside, returning to the scene of the abduction. Daddy was on my heels, chattering away, but his words weren't registering with me. All I could think about was how I would choke that darkie to death if she harmed a single hair on my baby sister's head.

"Doesn't it make you uncomfortable," I asked, "knowing Kelli's not here, with us?"

"It does." Daddy replied, "but this is the critical moment when we can't afford to overreact. If you activate the Combots now, all that I, we, have worked for will have been in vain. What assurances can you give me that they won't track the Combots back to us, you? You're the most renowned robotics engineer on the planet, son."

"I know that, Dad. And I know members of the Inner Circle are going to be furious. But what if something like this happened to them? Would they hesitate to pull the trigger, put this animal down? Not on your life."

I turned to see my wife Ellen exiting the house in a panic. She had called me during the fundraiser to let me know her connecting flight from Charlotte had been delayed. Then, after Selina crashed the party, I had to call her from an upstairs bedroom to let her know that Kelli had been taken. The two had been the best of friends at Ole' Miss.

"How did she get past the guards at the front gate?" Ellen asked while walking toward us. I would learn later that the front gate guards were the first to be taken out. "Do we know if she had accomplices?"

"No," Daddy interjected. "All we know is she had a power that no one has ever seen before."

Ellen's glare was scathing, almost incriminating. "What are you going to do, Horace?" The first of many tears rolled down her left cheek to drip from her chin. She wiped at her face. "That's my best friend. You have to find her."

She leaned into me, resting her head on my chest. I raked the fingers of my right hand through her blonde hair, using the other one to hold her close. "And I will. That's a promise."

Daddy stood behind Ellen. As I uttered these words, he shook his head no while making his way to the patio door. He probably knew the activation of my Combots was inevitable. But now that Kelli's tracking device had gone cold, I was on Selina's timeline. All I needed, though, was for her to make one critical mistake. SANDI would do the rest, as it was capable of patching in to any surveillance camera on the planet.

Catch sight of her on the street...

...at a restaurant...

...in a park...

and that would be the end of her.

I love my sister. That's probably why I was so willing to go against the Cabal's wishes by sending my Combots on a search and destroy mission. I created the Combots, with no assistance from our Satarian friends, so I felt I had a right to activate them when I saw fit. My sister's life was at stake.

Kyle Shuler is my father, but in my youth, I had been led to believe that he was my uncle. I knew my mother Andrea was adopted, so it shouldn't be a surprise when I tell you I took a pregnant pause after walking in on them while they were making out in my grandmother's walk-in closet. I was seven at the time. All I could do was say, "I'm sorry." I then sprinted through and out of my grandparent's bedroom to the guest bedroom that had been reserved for my mother and me whenever we drove to Jackson from Baton Rouge to visit.

I don't think it would have bothered anyone if they just came out and confessed to the world that they were much more than siblings. But knowing what I know about my Pa-Paw, he probably adopted my mother just so my father could have his way with her. Yeah, that's sick. Heartless really. But I never heard my mother complain. She was happy to be a Shuler, but even happier to be the object of Daddy's desire.

I was a college freshman when I realized that the foulness surrounding my paternity really didn't matter. I loved being a Shuler as well. But it was Pa-Paw who took me under his wing, shared with me the benefits of being white and wealthy. However, I also remember him expressing curiosity about black people, even saying they may have a more direct connection with the one, true God. To make matters worse, he once told me that he thought the biblical Garden of Eden was in Africa. He wondered out loud if Adam and Eve, the first man and woman, were actually Black. For this reason, he surmised, we wealthy Whites had to keep them under our heels so they would never know this truth, that they were first and not last.

My grandfather was the first person to make contact with the Satarians. He was a pilot in the United States Air Force, flying several missions over Nazi Germany at the height of World War II. On D Day, the day when the Allied Forces defeated Adolf Hitler and his storm troopers, his plane was shot down over Berlin. Fortunately for him, he was able to eject before Nazi missiles blew his fighter jet out of the sky.

On the ground in Berlin, he was captured by Nazi soldiers and taken directly to Hitler, who was hunkered down with his wife Eva Braun in the Reich Chancellery. The Chancellery was fifty-five feet underground, and served as Hitler's base of operations during his reign. But Hitler and Eva were not alone. Also present were four visitors from the planet Sataria.

Even though my grandfather fought against the Nazis, their ideas resonated with him. He rejected the idea that all men are created equal. Like Hitler, he believed White, Anglo-Saxon Protestant males were genetically and intellectually superior to all of the other racial/ethnic groups combined. Consequently, he felt the White race was better equipped to lead humanity toward prosperity. But the Satarian visitors told my grandfather a different story, one in which Africans were considered the superior race.

My grandfather told me that a Satarian named Jek-Saber shot Hitler in the head while in the bunker moments before the Russian military stormed Berlin. For good measure. That was April 30, 1945. Hitler and Eva had already been pronounced dead after consuming cyanide capsules. The history books assert that Hitler ingested the cyanide capsules and then shot himself in the head. The history books are wrong.

This story was shared with me after I graduated from MIT with my Ph.D in Robotics Engineering in 1999. I was twenty-one. I also learned that our Satarian friends replaced Hitler's Third Reich with the Corporate Cabal by using the occasion of Hitler's death to appoint my American grandfather the first High Lord of the Cabal's five-member Inner Circle. They wanted him to return to the United States to grow the Corporate Cabal's influence and control around the world. They even provided him with the blueprints to do it.

I pledged my talents to my grandfather's lordship. I developed devices and machinery that would help us exert more control over the Blacks if and when they were ever reminded of who and what they were.

Heil, Shuler!

CHAPTER 11
Jonathan Fraiser

When I returned to The Cradle, I told Mr. Black about what had happened at the dinner party, how Selina had taken Kelli hostage.

With Selina now being an assassin turned kidnapper, I knew Shuler's days were numbered. That's why I spent my every waking moment at The Cradle fine-tuning my fighting skills.

Our Adinkrahene trainers were proficient in an African fighting style called Jatube. It involved making slicing motions with your hands and feet, with all attacks being fueled by the strength of an individual agent's core. The primary move for blocking opponents' attacks was the Cross-Bow, where the arms are crossed at the wrists. Big Nate had told me that mastering Jatube was a must for Adinkrahene agents because it connects us with the pain and suffering, but also hopes and aspirations, of our African ancestors.

"They say karate, and other forms of martial arts, grew out of Jatube," Big Nate had explained. We had just completed a 14-mile run on the trails running parallel to the Potomac River. I sat on a large boulder sipping Gatorade from a bottle.

"What about all of those rumors?" I had asked. "About being connected to something called the Slipstream Grid?"

"I know what you know, bruh. And that's not much. I just hope we get connected soon. Selina's a beast."

"Selina is connected to The Grid," I said.

"Yeah, man. Probably one of the first." Big Nate rubbed the back of his neck. "Other agents have stepped up to teach us Jatube, but Selina put them to shame. Any of the other brothers will tell you that we were on the fast track with her. She knew how to make it plain. Still having a hard time believing she's no longer with us."

"Can you blame her, man?" My eyes bore into him.

"But Adinkrahene doesn't exist to exact revenge on white folks, Jonathan. Selina is violating everything we stand for."

"Well, I guess it will be up to us to protect the bastard."

The worried look on Big Nate's face unnerved me. "She's not going to hold back, you know? And if she's still connected to the Slipstream Grid by the time she's located, our agents are going to have a hard time taking her down. You ready for that?"

I stood up. "Don't know, bro'. I survived her initial attack. Mr. Black has the final say on my readiness for round two."

Upon our return to The Cradle, Mr. Black summoned everyone to the Level Seven conference room. I felt bad because the room was already bustling with a mix of rookie and veteran agents, and I was one of the last agents to enter the room.

"Good morning, brothers," Mr. Black exclaimed as he and Doc walked from the back of the room down the center aisle to stand in the front of us. "And sisters." He greeted Iris and the twenty-three other female agents in the room.

"Good morning, sir," we replied, in unison.

Standing in front of us, Mr. Black continued, "I want to congratulate each of you for completing your training. I know it has been a grueling six months, but you did it." He exchanged a knowing glance with Doc before facing forward again. "I invited you here to extend an invitation of sorts to our newest agents."

We heard a whirring sound and then watched as a holographic projector dropped down from the ceiling. "By now, many of you have heard rumors about something we call the Slipstream Grid. Well, I'm here to put those rumors to rest. You being connected to the Slipstream Grid is the final leg of your journey." The room went dark as Mr. Black and Doc stepped aside. "This short video will explain everything."

The first image on the screen was the Adinkrahene symbol, but then the camera tightened on a moving object in the center circle. The object morphed into a black male dressed from head to toe in an all-black combat suit. His black faceplate hid his identity.

"Slipstream technology is in its infancy," a narrator's voice could be heard coming from the Bose sound system, "with Adinkrahene's First Twenty-Five being at the forefront of its development." We then watched as the camera pulled back to reveal that the black male stood at the edge of a cliff, peering down into a chasm. "The Slipstream Effect allows Adinkrahene agents to do the impossible."

The agent on the screen stepped over the ledge and dropped out of sight. One of the new female agents could be heard gasping. But I just sat there, a somewhat stoic expression on my face. I knew how this story ended.

The agent slowly floated from the abyss to fly to the other side of the chasm. After he reached the other side, he turned toward the camera, and flashed the Cross-Bow. His body then let out a fluorescent blue light that pulsated all around him.

The narrator's voice continued, saying, "The Slipstream Effect – True. Black. Power."

The lights flickered back on, and the laboratory doors to our left slid open with a hiss.

"Members of the Final Twenty-Five," Doc exclaimed, with his right arm extended toward the laboratory entrance. "If you step this way, this power will now be yours."

Mr. Black stood beside his friend and colleague, his hands behind his back. The veteran agents applauded us rookie agents as they watched us make our way to and through the laboratory doors. Before I could enter, Mr. Black motioned me to him.

"Do you believe in Adinkrahene Justice, my friend," he exclaimed, his hand on my shoulder.

"Yes, sir. I do."

He removed his hand from my shoulder. "Good. It will serve you well. Just never forget what you're fighting for."

"And what is that, sir?"

"Restoration of the Pangeon Nation."

"Is this going to hurt?" I asked. I was lying face down on a padded table that was aligned with a computerized tomography machine. When I entered the room from the waiting area, Doc had shown me the small dime-sized disc, encased in a block of clear Plexiglas, that he would be inserting at the base of my neck.

"Not one bit," Doc replied. "But I won't be able to activate it until you're sleeping. Being connected to The Grid for the first time is a pretty jarring experience."

The padded table was on a metallic track. Doc signaled to his female assistant in the booth above that it was time to begin the process. She did as she was told, and the table slowly moved forward on the track toward the computerized tomography machine. Once I was in the machine, I saw two, three-inch needles slide out of matching panels to my left and right. They mechanically aligned with my head and neck, ultimately stopping about a half inch from my neck on each side.

"Good night," Doc exclaimed. The needles pierced the flesh on the sides of my neck, injecting some kind of anesthesia. After that, it was lights out.

The Washington Post presents
Culturally Coded
A Weekly Column by J.A. Fraiser

BENDING OVER BACKWARDS FOR THE FIRST, BLACK PRESIDENT

In 2008, America achieved something that political pundits said was impossible - it elected its first, black president. These pundits weren't racist or bigoted. They just knew the country was on life support, and, consequently, they didn't think Herbert Newsom's experience as a community organizer on the mean streets of Chicago qualified him to clean up George W. Bush's mess. But now that he is in office, you have to wonder if the American citizenry is ready to bend over backwards for the first black president.

The general consensus in and around Washington is that George W. Bush is the reason why the country's economy was on life support when Newsom took the Presidential Oath of Office in January 2009. The country was involved in two wars - one in Afghanistan, the other in Iraq - and the unemployment rate was hovering above eight percent.

Because Bush the Republican was responsible for the onset of these problems, you would have thought the Republican Party would have paid a much heavier price at the polls during the 2010 Midterm Elections. But they didn't. From the synergy generated by the newly formed Tea Party, the Grand Ole' Party (GOP) was able to regain control of the House while conceding control of the Senate to the Democrats.

But three years after Newsom's historic election, you have to wonder what the GOP and Republican Tea Party are thinking now that the American economy is starting to recover. American troops are no longer occupying Iraq. And in December 2014, additional regiments will be pulled out of Afghanistan. Moreover, the unemployment rate is at its lowest rate since before President Bush left office - 7.3 percent. Add the passage and signing of the Affordable Care Act into the mix in 2009, and you begin to see how this story could have a happy ending.

But stories also have colorful characters, and the one character that has not shown up in mass since President Newsom's election is you, enlightened America. As I watched the returns come in from the 2008 presidential election, I was moved by images of racially diverse crowds wearing NEWsom DAY t-shirts and sweaters. I could sense these Newsom supporters were hopeful that President Newsom and the Democrats would bring an end to the Republican Party's practice of rigging the system with legislation that made the rich richer, the poor poorer. What concerned me after the election, though, was these hopeful and enlightened Americans thinking President Newsom was a cure-all for all of America's ailments. I knew if he didn't deliver on something big within the first two years of his presidency, they would abandon him.

Because the unemployment rate had risen above eight percent under the Bush Administration, many of us thought President Newsom should have introduced a federal jobs bill. Instead, he introduced the Affordable Care Act, or ACA. The purpose of this bill was to bring the soaring costs of healthcare down and eliminate the practice of denying Americans health insurance coverage because of pre-existing conditions. Even

I openly criticized President Newsom for choosing healthcare over jobs. But then I started to understand why he made this decision.

Affordable healthcare is a right that the corporate sector has turned into a privilege. Under the old system, if you wanted to take advantage of this privilege (i.e., access the best doctors and the best treatment), you had to be in a position to pay high deductibles. And even if you could pay these high deductibles, you still weren't guaranteed coverage, especially if you had a pre-existing condition. So, after months of chastising President Newsom for what I called a "dumb move", I concluded that his decision was righteous, for its passage and signing has moved us closer to the day when health insurance coverage will be considered more right than privilege.

I saw you, enlightened America, out there occupying Wall Street. I perceived this act of defiance as you finally getting sick and tired of being trampled on by the richest Americans, or what many economists call the One Percent. I'm almost tempted to give you credit for bending over backwards for the first black president, but that would be somewhat presumptuous of me. You're not bending over backwards for any one man or any one party. If anything, you're bending over backwards for a more prosperous future. And you are willing to vote for any candidate who supports fairness, equal opportunity for all.

Just know it was your enlightenment that elected President Herbert Newsom as the leader of the Free World. You foresaw a Republican-controlled Congress opposing anything with President Newsom's imprint on it. Consequently, it is imperative that we enlightened Americans support President Newsom's efforts to transform America into a more perfect union. Not because he is the first, black president. But because he has shown himself to be the fairest and most righteous one.

CHAPTER 12
Kelli Shuler

My body was bruised and bloodied, but not broken. As I lay there, on the concrete floor of that dilapidated building in an oversized, iron-barred cage, all I could do was mumble a silent prayer.

They had stripped me naked and beaten me with sticks. Must have been five or six of them, all females. After they grew tired of whipping me, they had thrown me in the cage, which had been placed in the room long before my abduction. No sympathy for me, not even from the males. But many of these same males would enter the room in the middle of the night to get prolonged looks at my naked body. At times, I found myself shuffling away from them inside the cage because they would reach inside it to grope my breasts and thighs, run their fingers through my hair.

During the day, they would also sit at tables near the far wall playing Spades or surfing the 'Net on their tablet computers. The black females turned up their lips every time they caught one of them sneaking glances at me.

I did my best to cover up, sitting on the floor with my bent knees up to my chest. But because their faces were always covered with masks, I couldn't tell if my good looks pleased them. But the fact that their heads faced me in locked positions let me know they were at least interested.

The black females' hatred of me was obvious. During the day, they lobbed racial slurs at me - Cracker, Honkie, White Bitch. Pa-Paw would call this a case of "Nigra bitches gone wild." I wondered how people could despise someone they had never met.

I was lying on my side when I saw Selina. She stood in the doorless doorway scolding two of the male perverts. Her back was to me, so I couldn't see her unmasked face. The message that she was sending to the two men must have gotten through, because they retreated to another room.

Selina turned toward me.

I sat up as she approached so I could face her head on. "Why are you doing this?" I asked. "To me. I'm not your enemy."

Selina sat in one of the chairs surrounding the cage, her legs spread wide, her hands intertwined as she leaned forward. She was still dressed in the black, form-fitting combat suit that she wore when she crashed my father's fundraiser. An Adinkrahene symbol that I had not noticed before was stitched in silver on the front of the combat suit, above her left breast.

"What have they told you about my grandmother?"

I paused for a moment before replying. "That they found her body in a river, about a hundred miles east of Jackson."

"Did they tell you she was working for your grandparents the day she came up missing?"

"They did."

"What were your thoughts when they told you that?"

"That someone must have abducted her before she could reach the bus stop."

Selina slammed the palms of her hands into her thighs, and then stood up. She paced back and forth in front of the cage before rushing over to grip the iron bars. I jumped.

"I always considered you a smart kid, Kelli," she continued, releasing the bars. "Someone who could put two and two together. But you're as dumb as the rest of your family." The fire in her eyes burned brightly. "Your father, murdered my grand-mother. He's going to pay for that."

I fought to get to my feet and then desperately lunged for the other side of the cage. "But I had nothing to do with it, Selina. Holding me here serves no purpose."

My last statement caused Selina to stop in her tracks. She slowly turned back to me. I shuddered at the sight of her toothy smile, raised eyebrows. She was clearly inching closer to insanity.

"An eye for an eye. A tooth for a tooth. After we're done with you, he will be forced to come clean."

I slid down the bars and to the floor as she exited the room. My body shuddered even more from not knowing what Selina had in store for me. More importantly, I had my doubts that I would get out of this room alive.

CHAPTER 13
Jonathan Fraiser

When I opened my eyes, I realized that I was back in my room. My bedroom window was open, so I could hear the rushing water from the underground stream flowing through the cavern and splashing against the craggy shore. But I also felt throbbing pain coming from the now closed incision that Doc had made at the base of my neck.

"Welcome back to the world of the living." It was Mr. Black.

I looked to my right expecting him to be standing in the bedroom doorway. I waited, but he never entered the room.

I sat up a little straighter on my bed.

"Hello," I exclaimed. "Is anyone there?"

Silence, then, "We're here, Jonathan." It was Doc. "Just not there. We're in your head."

"How?"

Mr. Black said, "The Slipstream Disc implanted at the base of our necks allows us to telepathically and holographically communicate with each other."

Doc added, "You're now a walking smartphone, son."

They instructed me to put on the black, form-fitting combat suit that had been placed next to me on the bed. I was to report to the training deck. When I arrived, other similarly dressed agents, about seventy-four in all, stood at attention along the edges of the training deck floor. One of the trainers waved me to an open spot.

The training deck floor was the size of a football field, the ceiling at least fifty stories high. I started to step into the spot that I had been directed to, but when I saw Big Nate, I decided to create a spot next to him. He extended his fist to me, and I bumped it with my own.

The ceiling panels slid to the side, and we Adinkrahene agents watched as Mr. Black and Doc slowly floated through the opening and the air to land in the center of the training deck floor. They were also dressed in black, form-fitting combat suits. There were plenty of oohs and aahs from the new agents, but not from me. I had seen it all before, with Selina. I just wanted to know what I had to do to access the kind of power they were displaying.

"Family," Mr. Black began, pacing in front of us. Doc stood in the background, punching at the virtual buttons on his tablet. "The time has come for us to reveal ourselves to the world. For years, we have stood in the shadows as the Corporate Cabal has demonized us, members of the Black Diaspora. But I'm here to tell you those days are about to end. While we must still exist in the shadows, the time for us to exert more of our influence is now."

We all applauded at that.

"Each of you has been fitted with a Slipstream Disc. This disc allows us to telepathically and holographically communicate with each other, but, more importantly, manipulate the electro-magnetic energy around us."

We watched Doc toss his tablet into the air and then grab hold of it with some kind of energy beam to set it on a table twenty-five feet to his right, our left. He then pressed his fists together, extended his elbows out, and released a beam of solidified light from his elbows to his forearms that hit Mr. Black so hard that he was sent reeling across the room toward us. We scattered, thinking he was going to fall on us. But he didn't. Instead, Mr. Black encased himself inside a cocoon of electro-magnetic energy to freeze his descent and stand himself upright again.

"Y'all see that," he laughed, wagging his finger at his friend. "He sucker-punched me." He then raised his arm to fire two beams of solidified light at Doc. Doc erected a light shield to deflect the blasts.

Doc lifted his right arm to signify his surrender. The two men then met once more at center deck, where they joyfully embraced.

Mr. Black's attention returned to us. "A great philosopher once said, 'With great power comes great responsibility.' Seventy-five of you have received this power, one hundred of us all together. Now, you must decide how you will use it." Mr. Black then used his right hand to form a light-blue energy ball. We all became mesmerized by the sight of it. "I believe the most righteous path for Adinkrahene is for our leaders to move more of our people from mediocrity to excellence. Each of us must do our part to build upon the work of Douglass, Dubois, X and King."

He flung the energy ball toward the opened ceiling, where it exploded to give off something reminiscent of a fireworks display.

"But I must warn you, family. Misuse of these powers will not be tolerated. You must adhere to the Adinkrahene Way. That means you will not use this power to rule our enemies; you will use it to serve, protect humanity from itself. In short, you will use it to restore the Pangean Nation, where all of humanity is once again united in thought and purpose."

Mr. Black brought his hands together as if in prayer. "Anyone found guilty of not abiding by this principle will be removed from The Grid. Understood."

"Yes, sir," we responded, in one voice.

Before any of us could receive the Slipstream Disc and be connected to The Grid, we had to pledge our allegiance to the Adinkrahene Reparations Management Syndicate. But we also received a warning about the Slipstream Disc. Implanting it on our persons was the easy part. However, if it had to be remotely disabled by the ninety-nine other Adinkrahene agents due to an agent's selfishness, pride or greed, he, or she, would die instantly. To put this in layman's terms, a disabled Slipstream Disc was equivalent to having one's heart ripped from his chest. And we all know what that means.

No heart, no life.

Adinkrahene agents' hearts beat as one due to our connection to The Grid. Black unity at its best. But as I stood there watching Big Nate and the other agents gleefully swarming around Mr. Black and Doc, I wondered why no one had suggested that Selina be disconnected from The Grid. Selfishness, pride and greed were clearly motivating her disregard for the Adinkrahene Way.

Selina had been one of my closest friends, so I knew that if a vote came up, I would have reservations about saying yea. Thus, I knew I had to locate Selina, talk some sense into her, before Mr. Black and the others forced me to change my vote so her kill switch could be activated.

I really can't put into words what it was like when I first used my new powers. I just remember feeling a tingling sensation at the base of my neck, and then watching in amazement as streams of florescent green, electro-magnetic light oozed from the palm of my left hand. As I sat in the room of my Georgetown apartment, I stroked the bolts with my right hand as they passed in front of me. After that, weeks of training at The Cradle opened my eyes to its destructiveness.

"You think they'll ever allow a white boy up in here?" Big Nate asked. I had slipstreamed to the surface for the first time since receiving my new powers. I was accompanied by Big Nate,

Iris, Chantel Ross and Herman Gates – Strike Team Alpha, the team Mr. Black had assigned to me to ruin Kyle Shuler's presidential bid, expose his unconfessed crimes. Big Nate stood near the summit, staring down into the valley.

With a single thought, I commanded my helmet's faceplate to return to the disc. I then joined him at the summit.

The other members of our group removed their helmets in the same fashion, ultimately breaking away from us to explore other parts of the mountain.

"Don't know," I replied. "Would make sense, considering we're trying to restore the Pangeon Nation. Know a number of white people who share our values."

"Is what we're doing right, justified? Some of my best friends are white. But my involvement with Adinkrahene is making me question these relationships. I look at them differently now. You know what I mean."

I leaned back on a boulder, crossing my legs at the ankles. "Yeah. I know. Avoiding one of my white friends from church now. And he's married to a sister. Wants to get together so we can catch up. Keep telling him soon, but days have turned into weeks, weeks months."

"The two of you should meet. One thing I've learned about myself from being here is we don't have to compromise our values. All they want us to do is remain committed to the cause. I just question the morality of what we're doing sometimes, especially when other groups of people are being excluded. Doesn't that make us just as bad as the Klan, other white supremacy groups?"

"Probably. But they excluded us first, Nate. We must never forget that. We didn't create the laws that subjugated black people. Many of us just fell in line with their laws. They murdered innocents just because they viewed us as an inferior people. That's why we're here, bro'. To avenge their deaths, hold the perpetrators accountable for their crimes. And we have to show black folk how to stand up for what's right, fight with their brains rather than their brawn."

"So, we're now embroiled in some kind of race war." "No. We're taking it to the white ruling class, the one's pulling the puppet strings. Shuler's nothing but a pawn in the grand scheme of things. We know there's someone more sinister waiting for the most opportune time to pounce. We just need to figure out a way to get to this person. Take him out. That's the only way we're going to be free."

"Us Blacks?"

"No. Everyone. Blacks, Hispanics, Native Americans, Asians...and Whites. Whites rule because of their numbers, their using those numbers through the years to run rough-shod over everyone else. They rigged the system to benefit themselves."

"So, what's the play, fearless leader?" Big Nate asked as the other three joined us at the summit.

"We're traveling to Tampa in a few months for the Republican National Convention. Mr. Black wants us to bring Kyle Shuler to The Cradle for questioning." I waved my arms over my combat suit, and gestured to the ones worn by Big Nate, Herman and the others. Iris and Chantel were the first to bust out laughing. Big Nate and Herman just shook their heads with smiles on their faces.

Iris chuckled, "So, he's going to receive a visit from the Ghosts of Slavery's Past?"

"Exactly," I replied.

"And how do you think that's going to go?" Big Nate asked.

"Don't know. But if Mr. Black can get a confession out of him, that's another step in the right direction."

"And when he refuses to come clean?" Herman asked. "Because you know he will. That's one arrogant son of a bitch."

I touched the right side of my combat suit, near the hip, pulling a Holodock from the materialized opening. The Holodock was round, a little bigger than a quarter, but could hold over 1000 hours of holographic content. I held it out in front of me, in the palm of my hand.

"If that happens, we'll introduce America to Mr. Cleat McMullin." A holographic projection of McMullin's head appeared in front of us.

Everyone in the group smiled at that. We knew that McMullin's jailhouse confession would cause a media frenzy.

I continued, "Mr. Black wants us to put the fear of God in the man, let him know we know what he thinks no one else knows. Of course, he wants me to loosen him up by writing some complimentary articles about him for the *Post* that week."

"You comfortable with that," Chantel asked.

I smiled down at her. "Been doing it for over fifteen years. Can't stop now? Would look suspicious considering Adinkrahene has already made multiple contacts with him."

"He's a cold-blooded killer that should have been thrown in prison a long time ago," Iris interjected.

"Chill with that, Iris," Big Nate gruffly said. "We know what the bastard looks like under all that glitter and gold. But I see how Mr. Black wants us to roll this mission out. Elevate Shuler's profile even more. That way he will fall even harder, right?"

"Right," I replied.

"What if we meet resistance?" Herman asked. "We authorized to use deadly force?"

I replied, "Mr. Black doesn't think we will. They have no defense against what we're capable of throwing at them."

"What about Selina?" Chantel asked as she stood to walk up the hill. "Her trying to take him out while we're trying to get a confession out of him is going to be a problem."

Big Nate responded, "Y'all just concentrate on Shuler. I'll take care of Selina. I owe her anyway."

A longer than usual silence, then Iris asked, "What do you think she's doing to that white girl,"

"Wish I knew," I replied. "Kelli's tough, though. Selina is a woman scorned. Hard to tell what Selina will do to send Kyle Shuler a message."

When we slipstreamed back to The Cradle, Doc greeted us in the lobby. Concerned was etched on his dark face.

"What's going on, Doc?" I asked, my hand falling on his shoulder.

"It's Selina, Jonathan." My hand fell away as he placed his Holodock on one of the many long-legged tables positioned throughout the front lobby. The Holodock projected a holographic recording of Selina walking among hordes of people at Washington's Union Station. She wore a khaki trench coat, and her face was uncovered. We could see shreds of her Adinkrahene-issued combat suit peeking from under the trench coat as she pedestrianly walked to the station's central hub.

The city police and security officers didn't seem to notice Selina at first. But they immediately took notice when she stood in the center of the crowded station, her body engulfed in flames from having used her powers to burn the trench coat away. They surrounded her with their guns drawn, demanding that she put her hands up and kneel down before them on the station's tile floor. Selina looked like she was about to comply, but she jumped right back up to make an aggressive move toward the officers and security guards. Moments later, she radiated an electro-magnetic blast that disintegrated anything, and anyone, within a fifty-yard radius.

After the smoke cleared, Selina could be seen still standing at the center of the blast. Shots were fired at Selina by an army of responding officers, but each bullet was deflected by the force field that surrounded her.

"What are we waiting for?" Big Nate loudly exclaimed. "Disconnect her from The Grid."

"I second that," I added. Herman and the ladies didn't say a word, undoubtedly troubled by Selina's display of wanton power.

Later that day, Mr. Black requested that all agents report to the briefing room to discuss these latest developments. I sat with my team, knowing full well that we would be called upon by Mr. Black to do the heavy lifting on this case. It was then that I became overly concerned about facing Selina again. Because I was a friend who empathized with her pain during our college years, I knew she would expect me to give her unobstructed access to Shuler. However, my allegiance was to the Adinkrahene Syndicate.

Enough said.

"By now, all of you have heard about Selina Giles' abuse of power," Mr. Black began. "She is a member of the First Twenty-Five. Played a major role in the development and implementation of this new way forward.

Big Nate cleared his throat. Another agent in the back coughed. Besides that, you could hear a pin drop.

Mr. Black continued, "I knew her loyalty to Adinkrahene could never be complete until her grandmother's killer was brought to justice. But little did I know, she was forming her own team of African-American CIA, FBI and NSA agents. They call themselves Black-Out. We should consider them armed and dangerous. Selina, however, is their only operative fitted with the Slipstream Disc."

Big Nate spoke forcibly and boldly. "That's all the reason we need to activate her kill switch. Stop this carnage now. No one else needs to die."

I shot a few quick glances at Big Nate. He stared over at me under furrowed eyebrows.

"I wish that were an option, Nathaniel," Mr. Black replied, "but it's not."

"Why not, sir?" Iris asked.

Doc responded, "Because the First Twenty-Five function independent of The Grid."

We all looked at each other with cross expressions on our faces.

"If she's to be defeated, it must be during a face-to-face confrontation."

I asked, "Has anyone tried to reach out to her telepathically."

"I have," Mr. Black replied. "Repeatedly. But she's not answering my hails."

I raked my hands across my face out of frustration. Not with Mr. Black or Doc, but with Selina. She was now the ultimate terrorist, someone who could walk away from an explosion that originated not from bombs strapped to a vest, but from electro-magnetic energy generated by her body.

"We need to pray," I suggested, reaching over to my left to grab Big Nate's hand, and to my right to grab Iris's. Mr. Black smiled at me while Doc shook his head in agreement. "Only God can supply what we need to weather this storm."

CHAPTER 14
Kelli Shuler

I was lying on my side in a fetal position when I felt a tap to my shoulder. When I turned, I saw a large, black man standing outside the cage with a wool blanket in his hand. He offered it to me. I took the blanket from him, pulling it through the iron bars.

"Thank you, sir," I said, draping the blanket over my body. "What's your name?"

The large, black man didn't say a word as he squatted next to me on the outside of the cage. He was dressed in denim overalls and camel-colored boots. It was only when a sliver of light hit his face that I surmised that he suffered from Down's Syndrome. He just stood there staring over at me, a sad expression on his face.

"Marco!" another man's voice boomed from one of the room's darkened corners. "Get away from there. You know Selina don't like you getting too close to the prisoners."

Marco stood up and scurried away quietly to an adjacent room.

The man, another black one, emerged from the darkness, walking over to one of the tables set a few feet from the cage. He pulled a chair from underneath the table and carried it over to the cage.

"Mighty nice of Marco to give you a blanket," the black man said. He pulled a cigarette from its pack and lit it with a lighter. "I know its cold up in here, but I guess Selina wants your frail ass to freeze." He brought the cigarette to his lips to draw in the smoke and nicotine. "That's what your kind would have done to someone like me."

"I'm nothing like them," I replied, my teeth chattering as I spoke. "Some of my best friends are black."

"And I'm supposed to feel good about that? Honky, please." The black man then took a longer than usual drag from his cigarette. "Why y'all do that? Having black friends don't make things right. What did you do when the Supreme Court struck down Section Five of the Voting Rights Act? Applaud because you believe Republican legislators now have the will to coordinate fair elections?"

I had nothing to say.

"What did you do when President Newsom won the Nobel Peace Prize? Did you consider him worthy, or did you stomp around your office screaming, 'He's so undeserving. What has he done?'"

Again, nothing.

The black man stood up and walked over to me, to my side of the cage. Kneeling close to me from outside it, he said, "You let me tap that, and I'll see that you get out of here alive." He grazed my shoulder with the back of his hand.

I pulled away from him with a jerk, stumbling to the middle of the cage. The blanket briefly fell off of me, but I wasted little time getting it back on. "Get away from me! Pervert! I'd rather die than have sex with you!"

"Have it your way," the black man replied. "But don't say I didn't give you a chance. Who knows? It could have been an enjoyable experience for you."

We both turned upon hearing the creaking of a hallway door opening. Seconds later, Selina walked into the room with her entourage of black females. The black pervert seemed to once again dissolve into the room's dark corners after momentarily being trapped in Selina's gaze.

"How we doing today, Kelli," Selina asked. She stopped in front of the cage as the black females took positions to her left and right. The female standing to Selina's immediate right cradled a small suitcase in her arms.

"Look," Selina began, "I know it's miserable up in there. But I have to send your father a message. He needs to know that I can take him out at any time." The female with the suitcase turned to Selina while simultaneously opening the suitcase for her. Selina reached in to pull out a bullwhip fitted with a metal tip. "Even the people he holds dear." She reared back with the bullwhip in hand and then snapped it at the darkness beside her.

Ka-Pow.

Selina continued, "But I have one final message to send to Mr. Shuler before we let you walk out of here. Girls."

One of the black females walked over and unlocked the cage door. Once it was open, the other three stormed into the cage and pulled me to my feet. The blanket fell to the floor, and then they dragged my naked body through the cage door to one of the building's pole supports.

"Don't do this, Selina," I cried as two of the black females held me steady between them. The third pulled my arms around the pole to handcuff my hands together. Selina watched them, stroking the end of the bullwhip.

"Four lashes for every century my people were enslaved," Selina announced.

One of the black females interjected, "This b need to be hanging by her neck from a tree."

"No!" I pleaded, tears pouring from my eyes, down my cheeks. The three black females walked back toward Selina to stand behind her.

Ka-Pow.

Selina had snapped the bullwhip at me, missing.

She snapped it at me a second time.

Again. Another miss.

But the third time was a charm, for Selina at least. The metal tip dug into my skin and ripped it open like a hot knife going through butter. I could feel blood droplets sliding down my backside.

"Come on, Selina." It was the black pervert stepping from the darkness to rescue me. "One should be enough. Let one of us take her now. Shuler will know you mean business."

Selina used her power to lift the black pervert off the floor by his neck. I saw this as my chance to slip to the other side of the pole, so I did. When I looked up, the black pervert was suspended in the air, choking, tugging in vain at the invisible noose around his neck.

"No!" Selina angrily exclaimed. "One is not enough."

She snapped the bullwhip at me again, and the tip tore into my right forearm.

Again. It tore into my left thigh.

And again. My left hip.

I writhed on the floor in pain after each strike. I heard the black pervert land on the floor with a thud after Selina released her hold around his neck.

"I don't dislike you, Kelli," Selina said as she walked over to me to circle around. The pain radiating through my body paralyzed me. And as I kneeled near the bottom of that pole, I knew it would all be over with this one final lash. But right when I accepted my fate, the roof caved in. Selina and her acolytes scattered like a herd of startled cockroaches.

I lifted my head.

The unblinking eye of my metallic savior stared down at me. After that, I passed out.

The first person I saw when I regained consciousness was Daddy. My brother Horace stood behind him. Daddy rushed over to me when he saw that I was awake.

"Kelli," Daddy exclaimed, stepping closer to hug me. I had been transported to Washington Regional Medical Center, stitched up, and placed face down on a hospital bed in a recovery room. The attending physicians and nurses had configured the bed in such a way that kept me off my shredded back.

"How are you feeling," Daddy asked.

I angled my head toward him, as if to say, Are you kidding? Even though I knew the doctors had drugged me up with pain killers, the pain from my shredded back was still making my toes curl.

"And you thought those bio-trackers were a bad idea," Horace exclaimed. "The Combots would have never located her if they hadn't been inserted."

Daddy kissed me on my forehead. "Great having you back, kid."

"Thank you," I mumbled back at him, "for sending them after me, Horace. But I thought..."

"...the world wasn't ready," Horace finished as he walked over to the window to stare down at the media circus assembled in the outside parking lot. "Didn't really have a choice. They forced my, our, hand."

"But it's not them, Horace. It's Selina. She's out to destroy any chance Daddy has of winning the presidency." I looked up at Daddy. "She thinks you murdered her grandmother. Is it true, Daddy? Did you kill that woman?"

Daddy stood, turned his back to me. He then boldly replied, "Yes. I did."

My jaw dropped, and then the tears began to flow.

"Was young, stupid," Daddy continued. "Let my emotions get the best of me. But there's no bringing her back now.

Nigra's been dead for over thirty years. All I can do is stand my ground, fight back."

I reflected on the ease with which Selina had tossed Jonathan and Daddy's Secret Service agents to the wind. If only Horace could have activated his Combots before Selina crashed the fundraiser. Maybe they could have taken her down before I was carted away to be tortured. Who knows? But now that Selina's vendetta against Daddy was spilling over to harm innocents like me, I peered over at Horace for answers. He had sent his Combots to rescue me. Right then and there, I knew the innovations that came out of Shuler Robotics would be the American public's only protection against Selina and other super-powered beings like her.

Daddy squatted next to me, rubbed the back of his hand across my cheek. Then, as he peered over and up at me, he said, "She's going to pay for what she did to you."

CHAPTER 15
Jonathan Fraiser

"So, what are you writing about these days?" Tyler asked. We were sitting in a booth at a Crystal City Starbucks, about three weeks before the 2012 Republican Primary in Iowa.

"Profiling Cornelius Black," I replied. "You heard of him?"

"Yes, sir. Superintendent Hayes was thinking about installing one of his holographic projectors in the school auditorium. But what's so political about him?"

"Well, for starters, he's the Democratic Party's biggest supporter. The article I'm working on speaks to the legitimacy of Democratic dollars in comparison to those being contributed by Republican donors."

"That *Citizen's United* decision really paved the way for a corporate takeover of American politics, huh?"

"No doubt. And it's usually the minority party that uses underhanded tactics like this to rally its base. But there's something more sinister going on with the GOP. Most of the dark money being contributed to the campaigns of Republican candidates is coming from the Bain brothers out of Texas, and foreign billionaires."

"But Black should be able to compete with them in the political contributions department. He is the second richest man on the planet, right?"

"Right. But Big Oil has been good to Harmon and Nigel Bain. That's why they're fighting so hard to get the Keystone Pipeline approved. More money for them, and their investors, if they can find an easier way to get Canadian oil into America without having to cut through a lot of federal red tape."

Tyler abruptly switched topics. "How are you doing? Spiritually, I mean."

I swallowed hard, shifted in my seat. "Not as well as I know I should be doing."

"You attending church? Reading your bible?"

"Don't have time, dude. Always too busy."

Tyler tapped the table once, twice. "That's a pretty long fall, my friend. Especially after all that work Carmelita and you did with our teenagers. You two were great leaders. They miss you, Jonathan."

"And I them, Tyler. But things have changed with me. Don't get me wrong. I still love God. And I still believe in the power of his grace."

Tyler nodded. He was feeling me, but I could tell something else was bothering him.

"What's up with you?" I asked. "Things cool on the home front?"

"Couldn't be better. Just having a hard time dealing with the way people look at us, like we don't belong together because she's black, I'm white. But that's my wife, and I love her."

"And that great. But it sounds like you're allowing the haters to get inside your head. You got to stop doing that if you want to hold on to what you have. Look at me. I had a good thing, but I devoted so much time to being a great journalist that I couldn't see the writing on the wall. Carmelita is a good woman. And I allowed her to fall out of love with me, walk out of my life."

"Do you think the world will ever be free of racism?"

I sat up a little straighter, placed my elbows on the table. Images of The Cradle, the black agents training there, filtered through my mind. I knew right then and there that we would always be considered a black supremacy group if we failed to allow Whites and members of other racial groups into our ranks.

"Don't know. There are times when I really don't care. All I can do is me. But as long as you have groups of people who think they are better than others - the Haves and the Have-Nots - all of the -isms will be problematic."

"You know, Mary and I joined Living Water because of its racial diversity. As a white man, I never felt so accepted, so alive. But it was a different feeling growing up. I attended a mostly white Baptist church in rural Georgia, just north of Atlanta. Our lives revolved around that church. But our lives were so predictable, and boring. Seemed like we were insulated from the rest of the world. And if there was a problem in our tight-knit community, it was because of those people - Blacks, Hispanics, Asians, Native Americans. I know now that it was my parents, and all of the other conservative Whites that attended our church. They were the problem."

"Why do you say that?"

"Because they were hypocrites. They weren't true representatives of God's love. They represented themselves – their own interests, their own prejudices. And they were guided by selfishness not selflessness."

I heard the words breaking news, and my eyes shot to the flat screen television hanging on the wall behind Tyler. Sensing my distraction, Tyler turned to see what I was looking at.

An Asian news correspondent, a female with microphone in hand, exclaimed, "Kelli Shuler, Senator Kyle Shuler's daughter and Communications Director, was transported to Washington Regional Medical Center late last night. No word on whether the person who abducted her has been arrested. All we know is when she was brought in, she was weak and had deep cuts to her back, as if someone had taken a whip to her."

The image of a robot replaced the news correspondent on the monitor. "This is the scene on the wing where Kelli Shuler's room is located. Ten-foot robots patrolling the hallway, another standing by her bedside. No chance of another abduction here." The news correspondent reappeared on the monitor. "Back to you in the studio."

I reached for my satchel. "Sorry, Tyler, but I have to go."

"No problem, bro'."

I reached into my back pocket to pull out my wallet. "Don't worry about it," he exclaimed before I could even give it a tug. "I got this. You can get it next time. See you on Sunday."

Walking away, "Yep. See you then."

My strides were long, my cadence fast, as I waded through the media circus to make my way past the sliding doors and down the medical center hallway. When I rounded the bend on my right, I was immediately greeted by one of the ten-foot robots.

"Greetings, sir," the robot said. An African-American nurse watched our exchange through wide eyes from behind the nurse's station. "Kelli Shuler is not receiving visitors at this time. I ask that you return within the next forty-eight hours, at which time Kelli Shuler's condition will be much improved."

"I'm a friend, of the family," I replied. "I was with her when she was abducted. I just want to see how she's doing."

"I'm sorry, sir," the robot said as its hands went to its hips. "My orders are to keep this access point clear. You can join the others in the waiting room behind you."

I did as I was told. But instead of stepping into the waiting room, I ducked into the restroom. Once inside, I summoned my combat suit and faceplate. I watched in the restroom mirror as it materialized out of thin air, replacing my khaki pants and mock turtleneck shirt. I then slipstreamed through the restroom wall. When I passed through the open spaces and walls behind the nurse's station, I saw the robot flinch. It had detected me, but because I was moving so quickly, it didn't have time to react.

My slipstream through the hospital wall ended at Kelli's bedside. Kelli seemed to be the only person in the room, as the lights had been turned off for the night. And she was sleeping soundly, evidenced by her loud snoring. The soft light in the room allowed me to see the gauze and medical tape covering the wounds on her back. I cursed Selina for doing this to her.

I approached the foot of the bed.

Kelli's eyes fluttered open as she tilted her head in my direction.

"Who's there," she slurred.

But before I could reply, a bright, red light illuminated the room. I was then swatted across the room by a metallic arm. Lucky for me, I instinctively slipstreamed through the far wall. But my troubles were just beginning because the robot monitoring the hallway greeted me with arm cannons locked in the loaded position, pointed directly at my head. His once green eyes now flashed red.

The nurse had immediately jumped from her seat to sprint down the long hallway, totally spooked by the robot's aggressive movements toward me.

I slipstreamed through the floor, freefalling through about four stories of mortar, concrete, wire and wood. I heard a single cannon shot above me. I then halted my descent, slipstreaming to the parking garage, where I ultimately slipstreamed upward through the parking garage floor and into the driver's seat of my Honda Accord.

I slapped the steering wheel. "This is not happening." I then stuck the key in the ignition and drove away.

CHAPTER 16
Selina Giles

After those robots crashed the party, we fled to different parts of the city, agreeing to meet up at the rendezvous point, which was at a discreet location in Oaks Bluff, Massachusetts, the preferred travel destination for more affluent members of the Black Diaspora. Remaining in the Washington, DC area was out of the question. Cabal agents would be canvasing the city looking for us. And with the advent of these robots, or what I now know as Combots, I knew the Cabal had some extra cards up its sleeve.

I really wanted to whip Kelli's pale ass one more time, send a more resounding message to her father. Even though I admired the way Kelli was rising through the ranks to become one of the most respected Conservative voices in America, I still couldn't stand the sight of her. The male members of my Black-Out crew, however, couldn't get enough of her.

They acted like dogs in heat the entire time we had ole' girl in custody. Yeah, we stripped her down to her birthday suit, which was even appealing to me, but my black men should have known better. Black-Out has no desire to get in bed with our enemies; we want to overwhelm and overpower them. To me, that is the only path to gaining equity with the Whites.

Cornelius Black, my father, is a great man. I have nothing but love and respect for him. But his approach doesn't put the fear of God in people. It's a sign of weakness if you ask me. Restore the Pangeon Nation? After all they have done to inject fear into black folks' hearts and minds? That's not my style.

White Elites have been leading the charge to rake Blacks over the coals for centuries. Yes, the Satarian Empire has been pulling their strings, and its reign over them must stop. But the ancestors of contemporary White Elites gave their souls to Satan's minions under their own volition. If they had paid closer attention to the weather surrounding Earth's racial politics, they would have seen this storm coming.

What's that they say?

Oh, yeah.

Payback's a bitch.

I joined Trayvon on the porch. A few days after arriving in Oaks Bluff, we had our heart-to-heart, seemingly mending the rift between us. I apologized for taking a portion of my aggression out on him. But as I approached him, I could sense he was still feeling salty about the way I had treated him. He sat on the swing bench sipping at a steaming cup of coffee.

"Mind if I join you?" I asked, sitting before he had a chance to say no.

I reached over and touched his thigh. He flinched, crossed his legs at the knees.

"What? You still mad at me?"

He refused to state the obvious.

"I'm sorry, Tray. Really. I know how much Marco meant to you."

He nervously peered over at me, still cupping the mug in his hands. "He was all that remained of my immediate family. Our parents were killed when those white devils planted that bomb in the sanctuary of my father's church, remember? Marco and I, and a few others, survived because we were in the bathroom. Moma and the other congregants in the pews were ripped to shreds when the bomb went off. Marco was a challenge because of his mental disability, but he was my younger brother, and I loved him."

Trayvon's hands started to shake. "You don't appreciate us, Selina. We believe in what you're trying to do, but you have to start believing in us. This is supposed to be a partnership. And personal tragedy at the hands of white people is what brought all of us to this place, this Black-Out group."

"You're right." Silence took a seat in the empty space between us. "I'm just trying so hard to get his attention, make him react to what we're doing."

"And we admire you for that. We really do. But what's going to happen after Shuler and Baker are dead? Will Black-Out disband, or will we work together to take out every bastard that ever treated a black person bad?"

"We'll continue. We have to. You've seen the files, the suspects connected to all of those unsolved black murders. As far as I'm concerned, we have our hit list. All we have to do now is wipe them off the face of the Earth."

My eyes shot to the ferry gliding past us in the distance across the Atlantic Ocean.

"What about Marco?" Trayvon asked. "Those robots cut off his head, with a laser. He had his arms up. He was trying to surrender."

"Probably programmed to take no prisoners. Don't worry. We'll see them again. Your brother will be avenged."

"But they're not the only ones we'll see, are they?"

"No. They're not. Adinkrahene wants Kyle Shuler alive and behind bars. We can't allow that to happen."

Trayvon sipped at his coffee. "Is it hard not being with them? You were one of their first agents, right?."

"Yeah. There are some good people down there. All in it for all the right reasons. But Shuler's announcement pushed me over the edge. My father will have to take me out, because I'm not surrendering."

Trayvon's brow tightened. "Your father? Cornelius Black is your father?"

I stood, walked over to the porch's edge. "It's a long, complicated story. But yes. He is. That's why I'm still breathing. Hard to kill your own flesh and blood, especially when you're just now getting to know them."

"You think we stand a chance against them?"

I turned to face him. "What do you think? You were an Army sergeant. And your expertise in mechanical engineering has helped us create weaponry that levels the playing field."

Trayvon considered my question. "I think they're good. But you'll have to do all the heavy lifting." A slight pause. "Are you troubled by their unwillingness to put Shuler down."

"Not really. Their goal is to get all the races together to sing We Shall Overcome, rebuild the Pangean Nation. But that's not going to happen today, or tomorrow even. Probably not in our lifetimes. Not as long as the Cabal keeps feeding this belief that white people are God's gifts to humanity. They're not. We are all God's children, one no better than the other. I just want to expose and eliminate their leaders."

"But you know there are others just waiting in the wings to replace them, right?"

"Yes. I know."

"I guess we have a race war on our hands then. 'Cause white folk ain't gonna be happy after we're done."

"Not our problem. Don't see any of their political leaders advocating for African-American reparations, on either side of the aisle. But the Democrats are more reasonable, more sympathetic to our struggle, which is a significant change. Still have to keep our guards up, though. Like they say, birds of a feather flock together."

"So, it's Malcolm versus Martin all over again, right?"

A smirk followed by a smile.

"That's an interesting way of looking at it. But I guess you're right. Let's just hope our version of Malcolm's message is more resounding. Take it to the enemy. Win this race war...by any means necessary."

CHAPTER 17
Jonathan Fraiser

"What were you thinking?" Mr. Black lit into me as I stepped off the A Train. "You were instructed to not get anywhere near her."

"Understood, sir," I replied, "but I had to make sure she was alright. Kelli's a friend. Besides, I was geared up. No chance of them identifying me."

We stepped off the landing pad and walked toward the compound entrance.

"That's beside the point, Jonathan." Mr. Black sighed. "You know the importance of timing. They find out about us, or that you're one of us, and that's all she wrote. Kyle Shuler becomes president, and we have to put up with four-to-eight years of his nonsense."

"But what about now. You saw what that robot did to me. Almost took my head off. Can these powers of ours deflect bullets, bazooka shells and lasers?"

"Yes. And much more."

Mr. Black motioned me to one of the booths lining the curved wall. This area of The Cradle was a hot spot for Adinkrahene agents, as we often came here to cut up during our down time. I used this space often to write in my journal. The view wasn't as appealing as gazing down at the Atlantic from the balcony of a luxury East Coast hotel. But at least I was able to peer out at the cavern walls, listen to the stream flowing past the island.

Mr. Black sat first. I claimed the seat across from him.

"We're monitoring her movements. That is my tech at the base of her neck. I want it back." We both nodded at two swimsuit-clad agents, a male and female, as they walked past us. "We're sending a team up to Cape Cod to take her down, alive. May be the only chance we have of stopping her before the Republican National Convention."

"Alive? She's a loose cannon, sir. The bombing at Union Station was a warning shot. If you don't think she needs to be disconnected from The Grid, then she must be taken out."

"I will never order the outright killing of one of our own."

"But that's the easiest way to end this temper tantrum of hers." I shifted in my seat. "I joined Adinkrahene expecting fistfights. Not against white people in general, but the ones who have a hard time allowing everyone to have their own piece of prosperity. The real enemy has been revealed to us. We know now that it's not white people. Like Doc and you said, it's an alien presence that has caused unenlightened Whites to lose their morality. They are blinded by centuries of privilege, which causes them to look down on us rather than view us as equals."

"And that's why your trip to Tampa Bay is so important. The spotlight will be on Kyle Shuler. If your team can squeeze a confession out of him, that will strike at the heart of what the Corporate Cabal is trying to do."

"Getting that confession is going to be difficult as long as Selina is stoking the fire. She needs to be removed from The Grid, permanently."

Mr. Black's head snapped to me. "I can't do that, Jonathan." A noticeable pause as I looked at him bewildered. "I will never order the killing of my own daughter."

We both spotted Big Nate walking toward us down the back hallway.

I swallowed hard as I struggled to understand what he was saying. Mr. Black continued, "I know how much she means to you. She means the world to me as well, even now, when we don't see eye to eye. But I wasn't there. Her grandmother was. I just need you to bring her back to me alive. Let me try to talk some sense into her." A short sigh as Big Nate closed in on us. "You already book your flight to LA. Herbert is looking forward to sitting down with you."

"Yes, sir. Flying over on Tuesday."

"He'll be there the day before. I'll tell him to reach out to you after you check into your room."

Big Nate stopped in front of our booth.

"You alright?" he asked. "Heard you had a run-in with one of them Combots?"

"Bruised head, ego," I replied, "but I'll live to fight another day. What's up with you?"

Mr. Black answered for him. "Nate is heading up the Myrtle Beach Bombing investigation. A bus carrying over forty, black YMCA kids and their counselors blew up on its way back to Raleigh. Iris and two other agents will be joining him. We suspect the Klan, but we really don't know."

Mr. Black stood up and motioned Big Nate to his now-empty seat. "You brothers go ahead and chat. Jonathan, we'll talk later about that...that thing. I'm heading topside to tend to a few things at Holodeck." Big Nate and I then watched him walk toward a door leading to The Cradle's offices and condo apartments. "Nate, just put your operations plan in my box. Jonathan, I'll need yours by the end of next week."

"You scared, aren't you?" I said once we were alone.

"You can tell?"

"Yep. Just don't know why."

"They keep telling us that she is a living, breathing weapon." Big Nate looked away. "Don't know if I can beat her, man. Not in a real fight. She's tough. And now that she's tasted blood, I question whether any of us will get out of this thing alive."

"Why wouldn't we. Look, you went three rounds with her, on numerous occasions. You know her strengths, her weaknesses. You know how she thinks. You're better prepared than any agent here, including me."

"But her Ta-Roo is off the charts, bro'."

"And that's why Mr. Black is sending four agents instead of one. If you guys work together, she'll fall pretty easily. Just don't try to take her on alone."

I still remember how Big Nate used to mop the floor with me during the first three weeks of my training. I would consistently return to my room grimacing from the pain in my ribs, shoulders and back. I didn't know the first thing about using my creativity to manipulate the electro-magnetic forces that the Slipstream Device gave us command of. But night after night, I would sit Indian style on the floor to strengthen my Ta-Roo through meditation. I also used this time to practice offensive and defensive moves.

Every Adinkrahene agent's condo had an oversized training room equipped with weights, treadmills and punching dummies. I would place the punching dummy in the center of the room and pound on it with electro-magnetic fists. I did this even when I was hurting from a Big Nate beat-down. But the tables started to turn around the fourth week. It was then that I integrated boxing and gymnastics into my training regimen.

My reaction time improved. When I stepped on the training deck to spar with Big Nate, I tried to imagine myself as legendary boxer Muhammad Ali, but with electro-magnetic fists. I remember Big Nate throwing an electro-magnetic punch at me that probably would have knocked me out. But I seemingly dodged it in a somewhat casual manner which shocked the hell out of Big Nate. While I was dodging his punch, I created an electro-magnetic battering ram that hit him from behind and sent him reeling toward me. I plucked his body from the air as he flew towards me, and then body slammed him into the mat before pinning him.

Hulk Hogan, eat your heart out.

CHAPTER 18
Selina Giles

After about three weeks on the Cape, I longed to be in the city - Boston or New York perhaps. So, I decided it was time for Black-Out to spread out to other parts of the country to implement phase two of our plan. The 2012 Republican National Convention would be held at the Tampa Bay Times Forum September 1st through the 4th in Tampa Bay, Florida. I was intent on using the event to make a spectacle of Kyle Shuler's death. Live, on stage, I would rip his heart from his chest minutes after he delivered what would undoubtedly be a rousing acceptance speech. I would remove their White Knight from the chess board before he could dream of sitting behind a desk in the Oval Office.

I set my sights on New York City, which was a six-hour drive west of Oaks Bluff. I don't know what it is about New York City, but it mesmerizes and calms me. Maybe it's the Empire State Building, or the Theater District. I don't know. It was definitely a place where I could get lost. And that's exactly what I needed at this stage of this most dangerous of games.

Trayvon, on the other hand, was headed to Marietta, Georgia to meet up with Jim Crow criminal Harrison Forbes. He was accompanied by a team of ten Black-Out agents.

Forbes was only 49 years old, but Helena and her Black-Out Intelligence Unit confirmed that he was the mastermind behind some of the most heinous crimes against the area's Black and Hispanic residents. Helena's report said he personally draped the noose around Morehouse College student George McDaniel's neck from the bed of his pickup truck. He and a few of his deputies then looped the rope over an overarching branch before pulling the truck bed from under him. McDaniel managed to hold his head and neck taut for about ten minutes. But his strength of will eventually gave out. His neck snapped as soon as he relented.

The hanging occurred on February 13, 2007, three days after Herbert Newsom stood on the steps of Chicago's Old Capitol Building to announce his candidacy for the United States presidency.

It didn't surprise me that Forbes just so happened to be the Cobb County Sheriff. That's how members of modern-day white supremacy groups operate. Fake being upstanding members of the community so people of all racial/ethnic groups start respecting you, your decision-making, your service to the community. That way, when shit goes down, no one can call you a racist or a bigot. You can even accuse innocent residents of color of criminality, or claim self-defense after riddling their bodies with bullets.

If you're a White citizen, you can argue that you were "standing your ground" when responding to quote intimidating unquote black people, more specifically black males. Unfortunately, our black males were nothing more than moving targets for any unenlightened white person with a gun. It's probably a running joke among unenlightened members of the white majority to cast our black males as perpetual intimidators. For this reason alone, I had no problem giving them the ultimate dose of their own medicine.

"It's done."

That was the voice mail message Trayvon left on my iPhone. A video was attached, so I played it.

It all went down in a wooded area about 25 miles south of Chattanooga, Tennessee, right off Interstate 75. My soldiers wore black masks and gloves to protect their identities. It would have made my day if they had let the bastard see their beautiful, black faces. This was the end of the road for Harrison Forbes, who was still dressed in his Sheriff's uniform. After this, his right to life would be nothing more than an afterthought.

Trayvon's fist slammed into Forbes' face, sending red spittle splattering from his lips and nose. Forbes tried to sit up, attempting to buck up to his attackers, but Malcolm knocked his ass back to the ground, kicking him in his rib cage, multiple times, with his steel-toed boots.

"George McDaniel sends his regards, bitch," Trayvon exclaimed. He then accepted the noose that team member Malcolm Greene handed him, leaning in to drape it around Forbes' neck. As he was drawing back, Forbes spit in his face. Trayvon's hand instinctively went for the pistol holstered to his hip. Malcolm slapped at Trayvon's hand before he could remove the pistol from its holster.

"You don't scare me, nigger," Forbes defiantly said. "Killing me ain't gonna do nothing but make life harder for you."

"But seeing your white ass hanging from a tree is gonna do wonders to our egos," Trayvon replied as he used his gloved hand to wipe the spit away.

After that, the four Black-Out agents at the other end of the rope pulled, bringing Forbes to his feet. Trayvon grabbed Forbes by his collar to pull him close. "You're gonna burn in Hell for what you done done." He then returned the favor, spitting in Forbes' face.

When Trayvon turned to walk away from the carnage, the four Black-Out agents pulled at the rope once more, lifting the bastard off the ground by his neck. Frantic movements at first, but Forbes' body went limp after his neck snapped.

I smiled.
Kyle Shuler was next.

CHAPTER 19
Jonathan Fraiser

When I stepped from the tunnel to the gate, I was engulfed by a swarm of people rushing to either catch their departing flights or exit Los Angeles International Airport. "Sorry, sir," a burly, white man exclaimed, fighting to regain his balance after colliding with me. All I could do was nod at him, clench my carry-on bag a little tighter, and keep it moving.

I had come to Los Angeles to attend President Newsom's campaign fundraising event in Beverly Hills. Some of the biggest names in Hollywood were scheduled to attend. Spielberg, Hanks and Weinstein immediately came to mind. But the guest list also included musicians Jay-Z and his wife Beyonce', as well as actors Forrest Whitaker, Jamie Foxx and Kerry Washington. I even think invitations were sent to Sydney Poitier and Harry Belafonte. I had hoped Halle Berry would be in the crowd. I just wanted to get a glimpse of her, if not shake her hand for being so, well, fine.

To this day, I am amazed at how quiet black entertainers and athletes are about the issues of the day. You mention income inequality, and most of them cringe. They would much rather be talking about something else, as if the federal government was going to pass legislation that robbed them of their right to cash in on their celebrity.

But the ones I just mentioned know what's up. They know that income inequality exists, that it's more pronounced in communities of color. And it is this knowledge that motivates many of them to use their celebrity to draw attention to a host of social and economic issues. These heroes and sheroes didn't fear retribution from the entertainment moguls because they knew they were being used by them to persuade members of their race to part with their dollars.

When the Super Shuttle pulled up to the Hilton Regency Hotel on Century Boulevard, the concierge asked if I needed help with my luggage. I told him no, and then walked toward and through the sliding glass doors, my luggage in tow. Standing in the lobby, I made note of the people with name badges dangling from their necks. Probably a writers' conference that I undoubtedly would have been interested in attending. I shuffled to my right and walked over to the guest registration desk.

"Fraiser. Jonathan Fraiser," I told the Hispanic female standing behind the counter. "Here for one night."

"Yes, sir," she responded. "Welcome to LA."

She then proceeded to place my room information on two key cards before reaching over the counter to hand them to me.

"Thank you," I said, taking them from her.

"No problem, sir. Enjoy your stay."

I made my way to the elevator, but before I could hang a left, the same desk attendant cried out to me. I turned to see her walking toward me with a sealed number 10 envelope in hand.

"I'm sorry for delaying you, sir," she said. "But this letter was left for you early this morning.

I accepted the letter from her. Nothing special about it. Just my name written in cursive in black ink on the front.

"Thank you."

After I got situated in my room, I removed the letter from its envelope. It was blank. My first thought was someone was playing a joke on me. President Newsom knew me from my work with the *Post*, but he didn't know where I was staying. I started to toss it, but then I remembered what Mr. Black had told me, that President Newsom would be reaching out to me when I arrived. Didn't say how or when. It was then that I took a second look at the blank sheet of paper. The longer I stared at it, the louder the soft humming in my head became. Once-invisible lettering and numbers became visible – A-003.

"Hello, Jonathan."

I turned to see President Newsom's hologram standing in the space between my bed and flat-screen television.

"Hello, Mr. President."

"Glad to see you made it. How was your flight out of Washington?"

"Clear all the way. Yours?"

"Horrible. Hit turbulence the whole way. But we made it here in one piece. Been on the move ever since. Two fund-raising events in one day."

"And you're doing it again in the morning?"

"Yes, sir. After that, I'm headed to Iowa before returning to Washington, Marjorie and the kids."

President Newsom's wife was the former Marjorie Ubanks, a power-broker in her own right. Three years before her husband became the American president, she was the President & CEO of the United Way of Greater Chicago.

A graduate of the Harvard School of Business, Marjorie Ubanks-Newsom was considered a friend to the nonprofit community, someone who commanded equal respect from the rich and not-so-rich. But she turned her back on the six-figure salary that the United Way had been paying her to support her husband's 2008 presidential bid. After he won, the media fawned all over her. They also predicted she would set a new standard for what it means to be a sitting First Lady.

President Newsom's hologram now stood in the hallway.

"Congratulations on completing your training," the hologram exclaimed as it walked to the living room. "Cornelius said you have questions about Adinkrahene's future. Come!" It extended its arm to the love seat to my right. "Sit with me. I may have some of the answers you seek."

"...so I ran for president because I thought it was the best play for restoring what Mr. Douglass called the Pangean Nation. It's not enough to just be the President of Black America, or a diverse coalition of Americans even. My aim has always been to be a unifier, not a polarizer."

Thirty minutes into our conversation, I found myself standing, sipping from a water bottle as President Newsom's hologram sat in the recliner across from me with its legs crossed. One of the first questions I posed pertained to Adinkrahene's Afro-centric focus. While I admired the fact that Adinkrahene was committed to restoring the Pangean Nation, I was saddened by the fact that Hispanics, Asians, Native Americans, Jews and Caucasians had yet to be invited to the party. I explained that many of my white friends at Living Water were more enlightened about the adverse effects of racial politics than some of the black and brown people I knew.

President Newsom's hologram said similar rumblings could be heard when he was Adinkrahene's Supreme Commander. But he asserted that Syndicate integration was impossible. The Slipstream Disc can only be coded to humans of African descent. He added that the Syndicate's agents would probably be opposed to this idea anyway. Anglo-controlled corporations had too much influence over American politics, domestic and foreign affairs. Because these corporations had been running roughshod over the citizenry for centuries, and it would take more than government-led Civil Rights legislation and integrated public facilities to encourage unenlightened White Americans to give the darker-skinned groups their fair share of the nation's prosperity. They needed to see more Blacks pursuing academic and vocational excellence. They needed to see more black teenagers being attentive in school classrooms rather than running wild in the streets. More than anything, they needed to recognize the bad hand that they had dealt African Americans, and how their unwillingness to talk about it just made life worse for everyone.

"What are your thoughts about the *Citizen's United* decision?" I asked.

"A big mistake." the hologram uncrossed its legs and leaned forward. "But that's what happens when you have a long-standing tradition of being controlled by the Satarian Empire. Morality is thrown out the window. Now the voices of corporate executives and millionaires are more audible than the voices of middle- and working-class Americans." "

I watched as the hologram reached out to grab something that I couldn't see - a mug perhaps - and sipped.

"The hand of the Sartarian-controlled Cabal is in everything. It has long recognized that an increasing number of Earth's citizens are for diversity, not against it. Within the next fifteen to thirty years, Hispanics will be in the majority. Once this happens, the political party that they co-opted, the Republican Party, will be hard-pressed to win another presidential election. That's why they're fighting so hard in these local and state elections. If they can hold on to their governorships in the South and Midwest, they will be able to change the electoral maps through gerrymandering so Republican candidates will always be winners, not losers."

"But you're the president of the United States. Isn't there something you can do to draw attention to what they're doing?"

"No. There isn't. Not if I want to continue being everyone's president. It's up to the people now. They must speak a little louder, share their experiences with anyone who will listen. We live in a democracy. We must stay that way."

For a brief moment, we sat and stood there in silence. I didn't know what he was thinking, but I thought about the Corporate Cabal's ongoing demonization of Hispanics. Leading up to the 2010 mid-term elections, Hispanics were what some pundits called the new Black. The Cabal convinced the Republican Party's mostly White base that illegal immigrants had been registering and voting in local, state and national elections for years. Voter fraud, they screamed from the rooftops. The lie was so persistent that even independent voters opted to vote for Republican candidates. When all was said and done, the Republican Party had seized control of the House of Representatives, while the Democratic Party had held on to the Senate.

President Newsom's hologram continued, "What you need to understand, Jonathan, is there's this fear...this fear of a black planet. On both sides of the color line. Whites fear Blacks because they know what happens when you hurt someone, a group of people. They fear if we ever received even an ounce of power, influence, we would respond negatively, seek revenge against White Americans for feelings hurt, lives lost. But we Blacks also internalize this fear. Rather than collectively pursue excellence in all that we do, we buy into the White lie that we're second-class citizens, inferior, unsuited for more prosperous living."

Its index finger bounced from me to itself, and back again.

"We get it, though. You and I, I mean. We understand that all men are created equal. It is an idea that we believe in and work to make real. Not just in this country but in other countries as well. Our challenge is getting the buy-in we need to eradicate prejudice, discrimination and racism. We must dispel this myth among Conservatives and Moderates that America has seen its best days."

I flicked at the bridge of my nose as I returned to the love seat. "Mr. Black says Adinkrahene helped you become President. How? I and almost everyone in the presidential press pool thought Senator McShane out of Arizona was a shoe-in."

"And he should have been. But the GOP underestimated the American people. While all this talk about multi-billionaires being job creators energized members of their base, the fact that corporations were being counted as people infuriated everyone else. Couple that with Adinkrahene's underground messaging to Blacks and you had the makings of a winning campaign."

"Underground messaging? You mean Facebook? Twitter?"

"No. Undetectable texts and emails. You know how we roll, brother."

We both chuckled at that. I started to ask him how the Syndicate was able to identify African-American and African cell phone users, but then I just shrugged my shoulders and accepted the fact that nothing was impossible for the technologically savvy Cornelius Black. When you're able to discreetly siphon off fourteen trillion dollars from international corporations and governments without raising the slightest suspicion from city, county, state and federal law enforcement officials, hijacking cell phones must have been a piece of cake.

"What are your thoughts about Kyle Shuler?" I asked. I watched as President Newsom's hologram inhaled deeply and then flopped back in the recliner.

"He's going to be a tough one to beat," it replied. "But he has ties to Mayor Chase, or the man your own paper dubbed Mr. 47 Percent. Chase is going to be a liability for him. Most of his financial support will come from the Bain Brothers out of Texas and Sheldon Richardson out of Nevada. The Cabal takes care of its own."

"How will you win re-election then?"

"By believing in the American people. They know what's going on, and those individuals who don't like it are in the majority. But the thing I fear the most is these new voter suppression laws in Texas, Florida, North Carolina and Ohio. They could potentially dissuade people from turning out next November."

"Did he kill Mary Giles?"

"Yes. He did. I read the intelligence report."

"Will you be able to debate him with a straight face knowing what you know?"

"That's the plan. I just need Adinkrahene to set the table for me. Start floating rumors about his indiscretions and crimes. Get a confession out of him." A slight pause, then, "What did you think after reading Douglass's letter?"

"Hard to believe at first," I replied with a sigh. "But it puts things into perspective. Just wish they were easier to detect."

"The Satarians have corrupted our culture, Jonathan. People have a hard time distinguishing right from wrong. But you see what's happening now, don't you? Now that I'm the American president, leader of the Free World?"

"Yes, sir. I do."

"They reject every bill that Democratic legislators and I propose, all because they think the federal government should have a limited role in people's affairs. They ignore the fact that all my proposals were initially proposed by members of their own party, even parts of the Affordable Care Act."

"How do they get away with doing that? Political suicide if you ask me."

"I agree. But the Satarians' control over Cabal leaders is strong. As long as they can appeal to the white majority's racial resentments, they will always be competitive in local and national elections. By demonizing democratically elected

Progressives and their fair-minded policies, they add more fuel to an already out-of-control fire."

"Selina's not helping matters, is she?"

"No, she's not. The plan is for the Syndicate to one day reveal itself to the citizenry, let them know about the Satarian plot to rule humanity with iron fists. But Selina's quest to dole out vengeance on one man – Kyle Shuler – is going to weaken our appeal. The Syndicate will be viewed as a black supremacy group, and either I, or my Republican successor, will be forced to disempower it through use of military force."

"Would you give such an order?"

"Of course not. If anything, I would give Cornelius an opportunity to offer up an explanation during a press conference or some other forum. I can't say the same about my Republican counterpart."

President Newsom's hologram stood.

"I have to get some shut-eye, my friend. See you at the breakfast?"

"Yes, sir. Promise me one thing, though."

"What's that?"

"That you won't pass me over when my hand goes up during the Q & A."

"You have my word, Agent A-100." He turned to walk away. "Adinkrahene," he exclaimed before thumping his chest with a balled up right fist.

I mimicked his gesture. "Adinkrahene."

I blinked once, and then watched as President Newsom's hologram dissolved right before my eyes.

CHAPTER 20
Jonathan Fraiser

The 2012 Republican National Convention was held at the Tampa Bay Times Forum. I decided to fly in a day early for a four-night, five-day stay at the Hilton Tampa Downtown. Most, if not all, of the hotels were booked solid, as the GOP faithful scurried down hotel hallways and held loud conversations in lobbies, sitting areas and restaurants.

The other members of Strike Team Alpha were staying at hotels within walking distance of the Times Forum. Mr. Black thought spreading us out would be best because racial/ethnic diversity is not a GOP strong suit. He knew our being seen together would raise suspicion. We would undoubtedly be accused of conspiring against the Republican Establishment. But what would have been most damning was the fact that we weren't aligned with any of the GOP affiliates. We would have been looked upon as Progressive spies, strategically placed by the Democratic Party to say and do outlandish things to em-barrass the speakers.

While some Blacks have always been staunch supporters of the Republican Party, the fact still remained that the Republi-can Party was doing nothing to support the hopes and dreams of lower and middle class Blacks. If anything, the party used successful Black Republicans as props to denounce passage of the civil and voting rights acts. And when one Republican legislator after another stepped on stage during past conventions to rail against the scourge of illegal immigration, or used code words to make poor Blacks the face of the American welfare system, these successful Black Americans said and did nothing to replace fiction with fact.

Sell-outs.

When I stepped into the Hilton's 211 Restaurant and Lounge, I immediately made eye contact with Kelli. About four months had passed since her rescue, and by the looks of things, her recovery had gone well. But the scars on her uncovered forearms were still there for everyone to see. The same could be said about the scars that were on her back, the ones that no one could see. I knew the ones on her back hurt the most because they had received the brunt of Selina's bullwhip.

"Jonathan!" she shouted out to me from a booth. "Over here."

I made my way over to her, past the crowded restaurant's seated patrons. As I walked over to her and the two, middle-aged women sitting with her in the booth, I thought back to my visit to her hospital room, the one that occurred a few days after my initial one. She was happy to see that I was alright. The last thing she remembered before Selina dragged her away was me lying unconscious behind an overturned table.

Kelli stood to greet me with a hug and a peck on the cheek. I then sat, taking note of the two women's toothy smiles. Kelli would tell me as I settled in that Eve Jameson, a light-skinned African-American woman, was Mayor Chase's newly appointed Publicist, and Bobbi Newcomb, a Caucasian, was Arizona Senator John McShane's Campaign Manager from the 2008 presidential election.

"I have you down for ten o'clock tomorrow morning," Kelli confirmed. "He's looking forward to spending time with you." She reached over and caressed my forearm. "You're not mad because I won't be there, are you?"

"Nah," I replied. She had told me a few days earlier over the phone that she would be meeting with the RNC Chair. "But you have to buy me a drink or something."

Eve interjected, "I may want you to do a write-up on Mayor Chase. Having a difficult time resuscitating his poll numbers."

Kelli and I exchanged knowing glances. Everyone at the table knew Mayor Chase was a ship that had been taking on too much water. It would take a miracle to keep his political aspirations alive.

Bobbi said, "You're good, Fraiser. Every bozo at this convention should be hanging onto your every word. But I bet over half of them don't even know who you are, what you do."

"And I'm fine with that," I replied. "I just deliver the hard truths. It's up to them to open themselves up to what I have to say."

"We're open," Eve explained. "It's just some of us think you're full of shit. My parents used to tell me stories about how they and their parents were treated in the South in the 50s and 60s. That's why they moved us to Detroit. Life was different for us there."

I reared back on the booth's padded backing, probably to brace myself for the worst.

She continued, "My father started his own trucking company. Became a very wealthy man. Put six children through college. If it weren't for all those government regulations, though, he, we, would have had so much more."

"I don't think he was sweating from too many government regulations. Not then, and especially not now, in this economy. Last time I checked, American corporations and small businesses were experiencing record profits, with, I might add, a Democratic president at the helm."

Kelli interjected, "And now this same Democratic president wants to play Robin Hood. Take more money from the rich and give it to the poor."

"Which doesn't make any sense to me," Eve added. "You take too much from business owners, and you impair their ability to create those private-sector jobs that Newsom likes to tout."

I replied, "But the unemployment rate has been holding steady at six point seven percent for the past three months. Don't get me wrong. That's still high. But that's a marked improvement over Bush's numbers."

"Why are you here?" Eve asked, with a hint of sarcasm in her voice. Kelli's eyes shifted from me to her, and then back to me. "You don't belong."

"Because I'm a free thinker, someone who has never been in bed with either one of these parties."

Bobbi asked, "What's your position on abortion and same-sex marriage then?"

"Pro-Life. But these legislators need to stop telling women what they can and cannot do with their bodies. And who am I to tell someone who they can or cannot love? Last time I checked, God gave all of us the freedom to choose. We all will have to stand before God on Judgment Day."

"But he also admonishes us to make disciples of all the nations," Eve said, leaning in for what she probably thought was the kill.

"Well, I guess a majority of the American people just don't want to be Republican disciples."

"How you doing?" I asked. Kelli and I had retreated to the hotel lounge, where light, instrumental jazz music was being pumped through the speakers. Eve and Bobbi had returned to their rooms to prepare for the five-day marathon of speeches and late night socials.

"Scared. I know she's coming. Don't know the when, where or how, but I know she's coming. Probably already here. I fear it's not going to end well." She extended her scarred up forearms to me. "Anyone who would do this to a friend has no respect for human life."

"She must know something we don't know."

"How? She wasn't even there."

I took a sip from my wine glass, swished the wine around in my mouth before swallowing hard. "I'm just saying. She may have information that neither you nor I have access to."

Kelli stood, walked over to a somewhat secluded corner of the lounge. Two heightened chairs and a complementary table were in place, just waiting for us to lay claim to it. The multi-colored lights of Downtown Tampa sparkled through the over-sized window behind us.

"Gramps is too kind, too gentle. He would never do anything like that."

"But how well do you know your grandfather?"

"Not as well as I'd like. Just going on what my heart tells me. He's innocent."

"If that's what you believe, it must be true."

Kelli excused herself and walked to the restroom. It was then that I felt a tingling sensation near the base of my neck.

Selina was near.

CHAPTER 21
Selina Giles

I watched him from inside the back hallway wall, his head rocking forward every time Kelli said something funny. I knew he was faking the funk, but I wasn't mad at him. That's what we Adinkrahene agents are trained to do.

Smile.

Laugh.

Loosen them up.

Blend in.

Then embarrass the hell out of them.

The temptation to break up their little party was almost un-bearable. I knew that's what Jonathan wanted, to test mastery of his new powers against me. But I also knew he wouldn't risk revealing his double life to Kelli, or the other people sitting in the lounge.

A premature engagement would have also set Trayvon off. It was bad enough that I had yet to follow through on my promise to deliver one of the Slipstream Discs. The Mechanical Engineer in him wanted to study and replicate it. But we were close to putting the final touches on weaponry that would put the Black-Out Militia on par with our Adinkrahene counter-parts. But I knew the source of his impatience. The brother was envious. Why should I be the only powerful one in our group?

There were times when I wanted to tell Trayvon and the others about Frederick Douglass's unpublished narrative, which chronicles the existence of the Satarian Empire, the lengths it is taking to divide and conquer the human race. But I withheld this information from my adopted family because I thought it would deter them from helping me take Kyle Shuler down. Yes, the Satarian Empire may have planted the seeds that caused white Americans to think less of us, their darker-skinned brothers and sisters. But Kyle Shuler and others like him took the bait hook, line and sinker.

Disdain.

Disrespect.

That's the attitude their ancestors decided to take in their dealings with the darker-skinned races. And for that they should be ashamed, punished even.

I used to wonder if I could ever seek my father's forgiveness after I had finally driven a stake through Kyle Shuler's merciless heart. I applauded, and continue to applaud, the Syndicate's quest to take a leadership role in the reconstruction of the Pangean Nation. But I stopped wondering after I watched Kyle Shuler go on Fox News' nightly programs to reinforce the conspiracy theories that Republican legislators like to float about President Newsom and his administration. And I cringed when he spoke disparagingly about inner-city African Americans, how they are not taking personal responsibility for the trajectory of their lives.

I began this journey seeking revenge for my grandmother's death. But I now had Marco's death on my hands. Trayvon was now alone in this world. When the Combots attacked, he couldn't protect his brother because I had him suspended in the air. He will forever resent me for that, undoubtedly attributing part of what happened to my vendetta against one man.

"Hello, Selina," Jonathan's voice greeted from inside my head. A flinch followed by a smile from behind my faceplate.

"Hello, J." I replied. Kelli had gotten up from the table and seemed to be headed to the restroom.

"I hope you're not here for Kelli," J continued. "Because if you are, you're going to have one helluva fight on your hands."

"I'm all done with her, sugar. I'm after her father, remember? Hope your team is in position."

"It is. Just waiting on you to make that move. You're public enemy number one. A terrorist. Why don't you just stand down now. Turn yourself in so no one else gets hurt."

"You know I can't do that, J. Having too much fun rocking the boat. Besides, we believe the deaths of a few will sober them up to their crimes against humanity."

"No. It won't. You know two wrongs don't make a right. If anything, it's going to make them hate and fear us even more when the truth is revealed." He raked his palm over his nose. "He's one man, Selina. Come on, now. Stand down. Turn yourself in."

I took a few steps back as Jonathan's left cheek tightened, left leg jumped. The other members of his team were on their way to this location.

"Goodbye, J."

I then phased through the wall to stand in a deserted alleyway. After that, I took a deep breath before leaping from the surface to soar across the moonlit sky on a beam of electromagnetic energy.

CHAPTER 22
Trayvon Newman

We had spent a year and a half preparing for Kyle Shuler's extraction, and now Black-Out's best laid plan was coming to fruition.

Our operatives were embedded in the Hilton Tampa Downtown's kitchen, as well as its guest registration and concierge's desks. Some of them were even parking cars. Because Adinkrahene was tracking Selina's movements, we thought it would be best if she steered clear of the downtown area.

Every time Shuler and his entourage passed any of our embedded agents from the curb or during their strolls through the hotel lobby, our embedded agents would offer them greetings and smiles. Of course, Shuler never acknowledged them. He just walked through the lobby to the elevator with his cell phone up to his ear.

Black-Out's command center was set up in two rooms on the top floor of the Doubletree Hotel across the street from the Hilton. As I gazed out the window through my goggle's telescopic lenses, I could see Shuler's staff shuffling around in the background in preparation for the senator's mid-morning interview with Jonathan Fraiser. At one point, Shuler had the audacity to stand directly in front of his window, seemingly daring us to take a shot at him.

"Look at him," I exclaimed. "Standing there like he doesn't have a worry in the world. We should take him out now, before Fraiser arrives."

"No!" Selina's reply could be heard through my helmet's earpiece. "Nevel isn't in position."

Agent Nevel had been assigned to the Hilton's room service staff. He and two other embedded agents would be delivering lunch to Shuler's room, with a few surprises.

"Nevel and his team are in the elevator now," Rosalind announced from one of the adjoining bedrooms.

Helena added from the living room, "And Fraiser just arrived." Helena had tapped into the Hilton's hall-mounted cameras, and had been watching Fraiser the moment he entered the hotel.

With a single thought, I was able to bring Shuler and his guests into focus using my goggle's telescopic lenses.

Roscoe Baker opening the door to let Fraiser in.

Fraiser entering the room with a smile on his face,

shaking Baker's outstretched hand.

Shuler walking down the spacious room's long hallway to welcome Fraiser.

The three men retreating to the living room, with Shuler sitting on the love seat, Fraiser the recliner.

"Are you in position, Selina," I exclaimed into my helmet's microphone.

"About to land now," I heard her reply through my earpiece. "I'll let you know when I'm in position. Just make sure you're there for Nevel."

"Copy."

CHAPTER 23
Jonathan Fraiser

"Let me begin, Senator," I exclaimed as I sat upright in my chair, "by asking questions about your motivation for entering this race. It appears President Newsom's policies are working, as the unemployment rate has fallen below seven percent, and enrollment is set to begin for the Affordable Care Act in November 2013."

Senator Shuler sat on the love seat with his left leg propped up on his right, his hands folded across his lap. His black suit jacket had been flung on the back of the love seat.

"I believe in the power of the free market, Jonathan. I have spent my entire career representing corporations whose CEOs feel they have been treated unfairly by the federal government. Everywhere I go, these CEOs tell me the federal government over-reaches when it imposes more regulations, or requires them to pay more taxes. I'm all for health care being more affordable. I just have a problem with people taking things from prosperous American rather than making a way for themselves."

"I see. But after the Great Depression, the federal government declared a War on Poverty, subsequently creating a social contract for struggling families. What do you say to the woman who becomes impoverished after her husband leaves her and their kids to be with his mistress?"

"I think we need more affordable child care so these women can secure and hold on to their jobs, or enroll in specialized training to become more marketable. But I also think we need to solicit help from our churches, synagogues and temples. Faith leaders and members of their congregations must do more community outreach. Teach our young people how to sustain long-term relationships, enduring marriages between one man and one woman."

I tensed up when he made reference to marriages being between one man and one woman. Because I am a Christian, albeit a backsliding one, I share this belief. Marriage should be between one man and one woman. But I have always been saddened by the fact that so many bible-toting Christians are quick to judge individuals that identify as gay or lesbian. These Christians should just talk about the joys of being in heterosexual marriages. When all is said and done, God will be the ultimate judge on whether gays and lesbians are living and loving righteously.

"A few months ago, a young woman – a young, black woman that you and I know as Selina Giles – emerged from an explosion in Washington's Union Station unscathed. She reportedly was the source of the explosion. How is such a thing possible, and what would you do to protect Americans from similar attacks?"

Senator Shuler looked over at his Chief of Staff, who sat in a chair with his arms crossed. "I don't know, Jonathan. All I can tell you is we're still trying to understand what happened. My heart goes out to the families that were affected by this tragedy. But as you saw several weeks ago, we now have Combots that are prepared to step in and protect our citizens from this menace. As a matter of fact, I will be introducing a bill next week that will authorize the Secretary of Defense to contract with Shuler Robotics to begin mass production of these Combots for military operations."

As he talked, I caught sight of a white, spherical object – the size of a regulation-sized basketball – floating freely through the luxury suite.

Senator Shuler smiled. "That there is the SANDI model. Surveillance Android for National Defense and Intelligence. Doesn't pack the punch of the larger Combot model, but it does give my team a sense of security.

The sphere paused just short of the living room. It then shined an infrared beam on me.

"What's it doing?"

Roscoe Baker answered for Senator Shuler. "It's scanning you, making sure you're not armed."

The sphere chirped about four times, and then floated out of sight, to another room.

A rattling noise could be heard coming from the suite lobby. When we looked in that direction, we were greeted by an African-American waiter rolling a food cart down the long hallway and into the kitchen. He was dressed in a white jacket that extended past his waist, black pants and shiny, black dress shoes. Behind him were two similarly dressed waitresses – one African American, the other Hispanic. Hot on their heels were other members of Senator Shuler's campaign staff, who, once they got a whiff of the food, funneled into the kitchen from the adjoining bedrooms.

The African-American waiter rushed to take the food from the cart to place it on the kitchen island. He left it to his female colleagues to neatly arrange it on the counter.

"Should we continue," I asked, "or do you want to get a bite to eat?"

"We probably should get a bite to eat," Senator Shuler replied. "If we don't, we'll be licking crumbs from the plates and bowls."

Baker chuckled at that as he allowed us to pass him. He then fell in lockstep with us as we made our way toward the kitchen.

As I reached to grab a plastic plate from the stack, my hand grazed that of the Hispanic waitress. "So sorry, sir," she exclaimed, quickly pulling her hand away.

"No problem," I replied, winking at her for good measure, seemingly on the sly. She smiled up at me. Her teeth were so straight and white. I could also feel myself becoming enthralled by her good looks.

None of this went unnoticed by Baker, who belted out a loud grunt as he passed me carrying a plate of food and a cup of sweet, iced tea.

My attention shifted back to Senator Shuler.

"Voter suppression on the part of the Republican Party," I began. "Fact or fiction?"

Senator Shuler replied, "Fiction. Most definitely. These new laws are designed to prevent voter fraud."

"But study after study has shown that voter fraud has never been a problem. Why create a solution for a problem that doesn't exist?"

"Because it's the right thing to do." Senator Shuler used thongs to grab a chicken breast from the dish, drop it onto his plate. "Can you hold off on the questions until we get back to our seats? Remember, this interview was my idea. I'm exclusively yours through the afternoon hours. Okay?"

"Okay."

Sitting in our seats again, we engaged in small talk as we ate our food. He commended me for coming by the hospital to see Kelli. I told him about our dinner meeting the night before. Told him that she was looking good. He shared that his wife hated that she couldn't be present for this interview. It had been over ten years since we saw each other last, and she still had fond memories about the visit I made to their Jacksonville home.

I glanced over at the people in the far room. Roscoe Baker and a few other members of Senator Shuler's staff were crowded in front of a flat-screen television.

"Kyle," Baker exclaimed. Senator Shuler's back was to the crowd, so he had to scoot to the edge of the seat to turn and face Baker. "You may want to see this."

When he caught sight of the carnage on the screen, he gasped. An entire parking structure at the Tampa Bay International Airport had collapsed. And it wasn't by accident. Selina could be seen rising from the rubble, throwing electro-magnetic charges at responding squad cars, fire trucks and other emergency vehicles as hordes of people scampered away. Explosions everywhere.

A tingling sensation at the base of my neck.

"We got this," Big Nate's voice boldly exclaimed in my head. "Protect Senator Shuler."

But then, out of the corner of my eye, I saw some kind of device slide from the African-American waiter's right sleeve. The device had a red button that he pressed with his thumb. After that, I felt myself getting drowsy. But not before seeing Senator Shuler, Roscoe Baker and his staff slump in their chairs, drop to the tile floor like falling timber.

I heard multiple thumps on the side of the building, followed by the sound of glass shattering. Then booted foot soldiers could be heard scampering through the room.

I lifted my arm in an attempt to encase Senator Shuler in an electro-magnetic cocoon. But the grogginess in my head impaired my ability to concentrate. A booted foot then slammed down hard on my extended hand. I looked up to see a black man dressed in beige military fatigues, laser cannons attached to his forearms. Goggles covered his eyes.

"Put Shuler and Baker in the harnesses," I heard the man say as his foot pressed down harder on my hand. I could feel myself falling into a deep sleep.

"What about Fraiser?" another similarly dressed man asked. "Should we take him or leave him."

"Leave him," the first man replied. "We have what we came for."

CHAPTER 24
Selina Giles

The electro-magnetic burst hit me from above, sending me reeling head over heels toward the rubble below. Luckily, my body was in flight, so an electro-magnetic energy field surrounded my body. Without this layer of protection, I would have died from the sheer force of the blow.

It wasn't like I didn't know they would come. That was part of the plan. But the agent who fired the burst wanted to take me out in one fail swoop.

Great seeing you again too, Nate.

As I rose from the rubble, I looked up to see the four Adinkrahene agents descending upon me. Their faces were covered by their black face plates, so I didn't know their identities at first. But I knew the one in the lead was Big Nate. All I had to do now was single him out, because, for me, he represented their Achilles heel.

They hovered to positions to my left and right, front and rear, their arms pointed at me, ready to fire off more electro-magnetic charges.

"Stand down, Selina," Big Nate ordered. "We have been instructed to take you back to The Cradle."

I replied, "To do what? Let my father remove my disc? Not gonna happen."

Big Nate's face plate dissolved to reveal his eyes, nose and mouth.

"Come on, Selina. You're one of us. We don't want to fight you. You can't continue doing what you're doing."

"Do you even know what I'm doing, Nate? Huh? What we're doing? We're letting the world know the truth, that black people are the chosen." My right hand turned upwards to create an energy ball. "We are direct descendants of Eden, heirs to great, charismatic leadership. We have always possessed great power. It is now time for the world to see us for who we are."

Iris' face plate dissolved to reveal her eyes, nose and mouth. "We hear you, girl. But, like they say, with great power comes great responsibility. Guided by love, not hate. That's the only way they're going to respect us."

"And no one is respecting you right now," Big Nate interjected. "Not after what you did to that white girl, those officers and guards at the train station."

For a brief moment, I found myself mulling over their words. I thought back to the times when I visited Iris's school for lunch meetings, how I was impressed by what she and her staff were doing to help black children and youths become more than whom they were. I told myself that I didn't want to fight her. She was a friend, once my best friend perhaps. Even then, I loved her like a sister.

But I also knew her being on Jonathan's strike team wasn't just a coincidence. My father knew Iris and I were tight. Who better than Iris Banks to talk me into surrendering?

"They chose to sleep with the enemy," I declared, "not us. And all the enemy is doing is getting stronger. We need to hit them now. Hit them hard."

"And we are, Selina," Herman interjected as his face plate dissolved to reveal everything above his neck. "I know the place you're speaking from, because I was once there. Never been a fan of slow and deliberate. Our white brothers and sisters have been brazen, not fully understanding the importance of thriving and surviving together as a human race. But we're supposed to be better than that."

Chantel added, "We swore an oath," Selina. To weed out Jim Crow criminals. To protect this world against the Satarian Empire's imminent assault. It doesn't make sense to attack our own."

"But how do you know? How do any of you know who they are? Does your disc allow you to see beyond the veil? Mine does. And every police officer and security guard that I disintegrated in Union Square was possessed by Satarian soldiers."

"But none of that applied to Kelli Shuler," Big Nate exclaimed. "Did it? You locked her up in a cage, used a bullwhip on her. A bullwhip. You had no right to do that. She didn't do anything wrong."

Big Nate's jaw twitched after that, but only for a brief second.

Herman added, "And that doesn't make it okay to disintegrate their host bodies. Those bodies belonged to innocent human beings."

"Host bodies with Satarian souls, Herman. Their human souls were already with Satan."

I extended my arms to make a T and then proceeded to spin in the air until I could no longer be seen by the naked eye. This centrifugal maneuver allowed me to charge my Ta-Roo with even more electro-magnetic energy. I then released it on them.

But they had already encased themselves in protective cocoons. Consequently, my energy wave just rolled past them. Fortunately for me, it wreaked havoc on the airplanes flying in holding patterns in the space behind us.

"Herman," Big Nate barked. "Iris. Get those planes on the ground safely. Chantel, go help the emergency personnel below pull people from the rubble. I'll take care of our...our..rogue agent."

He then performed a thunder clap maneuver that would have rung my bell if I had been caught in its wave. But rather than fight, I fled, pressing my legs together, arms to my sides, to propel my body higher into the late afternoon sky. Big Nate pursued me.

After jetting through about fifty miles of airspace, I flipped to my back and fired two electro-magnetic energy blasts at him. He dodged both.

Impressive.

During our sparring sessions at the mansion or in The Cradle, the brother proved to be bullish when circumstances required him to be deliberate. However, I was even more impressed by his ability to create an electro-magnetic battering ram that slammed into my body from behind. The move caught me by surprise, and the force of the blow caused me to lose my bearings. That's all the time he needed to snap one of my father's Inhibitor Collars around my neck. Once that was done, he used his telekinesis to restrain and suspend me in the air.

"Bastard," I spat as he reeled me in.

Big Nate didn't offer a response.

The smile on his face spoke volumes.

I rolled from my back to my side, and then sat upright on the floor, which was coated with shards of broken glass. The luxury suite was abuzz with activity, as detectives, officers and hotel management questioned the conscious members of Senator Shuler's staff. Paramedics also treated those individuals who had sustained cuts during the assault. Fortunately for me, the only injury I had sustained was to my ego.

As I stood, I reached out to Big Nate with my mind.

"Status report!" I barked.

"We have her in custody," I heard Big Nate reply in my head. "The A Train is in route." A slight pause, and then Big Nate stated the obvious. "They have Shuler, don't they?"

"Yep. Baker too. Mr. Black is not going to be happy."

"What happened?"

"The food. Must have put something in it. A depressant that activates when exposed to an electric current. Something Selina done cooked up for her cronies."

"Any leads?"

"Yeah. The restaurant staff definitely had something to do with it. Sending you the memories now."

I blinked three times, sending the team my memories of the African-American waiter and his two female accomplices. I thought about sending memories of the Black-Out operatives' assault on the suite, but they would have been of no use. All of the operatives were dressed in beige fatigues, and their faces were covered with stockings and goggles. However, I knew Mr. Black and Doc would want to conduct a more thorough analysis of my memories upon our return to The Cradle.

"Welcome home," Mr. Black said as Iris and Chantel led Selina off the A Train in handcuffs and onto the landing platform.

Selina replied, "Can't say I'm going to enjoy being here, but it's all good. We won. Beat you bastards at your own game."

The first thing Big Nate and I heard upon exiting the shuttle was "We won."

"There are no winners here, Selina," I said. "Only losers."

"Well, Shuler and Baker are going to be two of the biggest losers if you don't release me. My team has its orders. And it will execute those orders whether you release me or not."

Big Nate cut in. "You can't be serious. Not after what you did at the airport, to those people."

"My agents could have handed you over to the authorities, Selina," my father said, "but they didn't. They didn't because you need help. The kind of help only we can provide." He then directed Iris and Chantel to take her to the brig.

"One thing I will say about her," Doc began. My team and I were seated around a table in one of The Cradle's small conference rooms for an impromptu debrief session. A holographic representation of the most vocal Black-Out soldier rotated above a plate-sized Holodock. "She knows how to assemble a team." He then looked directly at me. "First thing she did was hire a few trained scientists and mechanical engineers. Love the design for those arm-mounted laser cannons. Our electromagnetic shields are going to be put to the test if and when we engage them in combat."

"Here's hoping our shields pass the test then," Mr. Black proclaimed from the other side of the table. "But we have to stamp them out before they take away any chance we have of quelling white resentment."

"What's our next play, sir?" I asked. "If we don't locate them soon, they're as good as dead."

Mr. Black raked his hand across his face, and then reared back in his chair.

"Never in my wildest dreams did I think she would betray us like this," he exclaimed. "The Corporate Cabal now knows what we can do. They're going to hit us hard, probably send the United States military after us. Going to be hard for them to believe that we exist to protect them, not harm them. Therefore, our only option is to bring Kyle Shuler back to his family...alive."

"What about his crimes, sir?" Iris interjected. "Doesn't he deserve some kind of punishment for what he did to Selina's grandmother?"

"Yes, he does, Iris. But we are neither judge nor jury. Our primary objective has always been to prevent him from becoming president. Now that he has been captured by what should be considered the most formidable terrorist organization on the planet, we must make a good faith effort to rescue him."

"He just doesn't understand how much Granny meant to me."

Those were the words that came out of Selina's mouth as I sat outside her cell in the brig. She sat Indian style on the only piece of furniture in her cell, a cot.

I had wanted to visit her immediately after my team's debriefing session with Mr. Black and Doc, but I thought it would be best if I allowed her to stew a little, think about the consequences of her actions. This lasted all but forty-eight hours, then I said enough is enough. But based on her demeanor and response, I could tell it would take something more than a lecture from me to cure her of her tunnel vision.

"I understood," I offered. "And I was willing to do anything you needed to take down the person who slit her throat, dumped her body in the river. But this vendetta that you have against him is over the top." I paced a couple of times in front of the Plexiglas wall between freedom and imprisonment. "I get it. You have tapped into something that allows you to see them for who they are. But the world isn't going to see things the way you see them. All they see is an angry black woman murdering what they think are innocent white folk."

Selina tugged at a string on her bed linen. I could tell she was carefully considering my words, but I also knew she had visions of Kyle Shuler lying in a pool of blood.

"Did you know I allowed myself to get close to him, his family, because I wanted to see him for who he is? They're not possessed like the others. Their human souls still abide in their physical bodies. That scares the hell out of me. It should scare the hell out of you too."

"Why?"

"Because it lets us know they made a pact with the Devil, or, at the very least, his Satarian creations. They probably made it thinking they would get something in return."

I stood there with my arms crossed. Her points were valid. As far as we Adinkrahene agents knew, no one in the Corporate Cabal was under Satarian possession. Therefore, their greed continued to be fueled by the collective ambition of subverting the world's darker skinned groups.

"Mr. Black and Doc seem to think a vast majority of them can be saved."

"I think that too. But the chances of that happening are getting slimmer each day. What the Corporate Cabal is doing is inexcusable. They're stoking white resentment just because the country is being led by the first African-American president.

President Newsom believes in fairness, justice and equality across the board. He could go down as one of America's greatest leaders, if not the greatest. But they're opposing him at every turn because they wouldn't be able to live with themselves if he and Democratic legislators made prosperity real for everyone instead of for a select few."

"And what you're doing is helping how?" I asked, uncrossing my arms to lock them behind my back. "Adinkrahene was about to break the Corporate Cabal's influence over unenlightened Whites. If it weren't for enlightened Whites, Herbert Newsom wouldn't be president now. Your temper tantrum, quest to take out one man, may have ruined any chance America has of electing another president of color. I don't know about you, but I wouldn't be able to live with myself if that happened."

Our eyes locked for what seemed like an eternity. But then I saw the tears welling up in her eyes. Looking away from me, she wiped at the wetness on her cheeks. It was then that I looked away, chastising myself a little for being so harsh with her.

"You know I love you like a sister," I declared.

Selina slowly lifted her head, fresh tears glistening on her cheeks and chin.

"And...and..I love you...like a brother," she reluctantly replied.

"Adinkrahene?"

Her hands went to her face, erasing the wetness. A devious smile followed. "No, no, my brother. Black-Out."

END OF BOOK ONE

ABOUT THE AUTHOR

J. A. Faulkerson is Northern Virginia-based Creative Writer who has penned instant classics like *Adinkrahene: Fear of a Black Planet* (fiction), *Real Men Raise CHAMPIONS: Unleashing Your Inner COACH* (nonfiction) and *Young Achiever Playbook: Planning To Achieve (nonfiction)*. In July 2015, *Adinkrahene: Fear of a Black Planet* was named one of three finalists for a **Phillis Wheatley Book Award** (in the First Fiction category). The **Phillis Wheatley Book Awards** are held annually as the kickoff event for New York City's **Harlem Book Fair**.

J. A. is available to speak about his insights and experiences as a Creative Writer, Child and Family Advocate, Social Entrepreneur, and former TRIO Upward Bound and YMCA Director.

Stay tuned for the next two books in
J. A. Faulkerson's
Adinkrahene Novel Series

BOOK TWO
Fear of a Beloved Community

BOOK THREE
Fear of an Alien Presence

THE ART OF

ADINKRAHENE

Illustrations by
Demar Douglas, The Painter of Dreams
www.demardouglas.com

© 2014 by Jeffery A. Faulkerson.
All rights reserved.

AGENT JONATHAN FRAISER

COMBOT

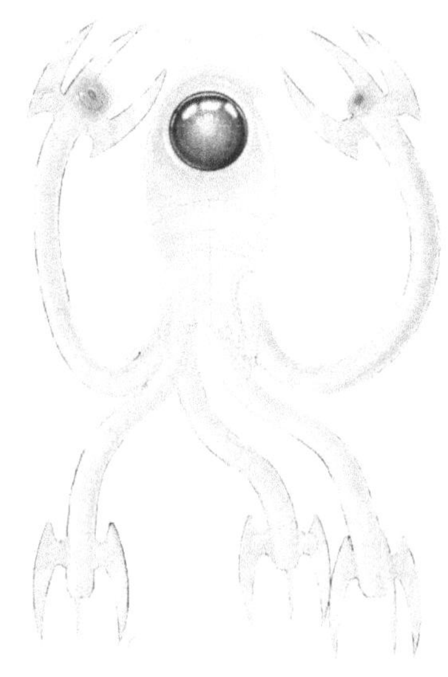